THE
FINAL
ACT

A NOVEL

Inspired by a True Story

THE FINAL ACT

A NOVEL

GARY M. CIANCI

THE FINAL ACT

Published by Marblestone Press
eBook ISBN: 978-1-7379870-3-1
Paperback ISBN: 978-1-7379870-2-4

The Final Act
Design by Rick Schroeppel, www.BookCoverDesign.us

DEDICATION

To the young college coed whose life was violently taken, but who has not been forgotten.

ACKNOWLEDGEMENTS

A special thank-you to the following:

My daughter, Suzanna, for researching locations on site, which enabled me to write detailed descriptions of settings. This background work could not have been done without her.

Robyn Huss, at www.HussEditing.com, for her solid editing, especially streamlining the narrative and dialogue to provide a fast and compelling read. Working with Robyn was friendly and efficient.

Rick Schroeppel, at www.bookcoverdesign.us, for creating eye-popping front and back cover designs as well the interior design. All collaborations with Rick were easy and productive.

Angie Lovell, for her ongoing assistance, particularly helping to discover the novel's editor and book cover designer, both of whom were a real find in the creative process. Angie also facilitated the novel's printing and publishing.

Carla Price, who served as my primary reader, made content recommendations, and encouraged me to continue writing the manuscript to completion.

My wife, Anna Patricia; my younger daughter, Julianne; and our family dog, Minnie, for their general support.

FOR THE READERS

This is a story of historical facts and fiction. The line between both literary devices has been blurred so the plot develops seamlessly—making the fiction as believable as the facts!

ONE

WHO'S THAT KNOCKING
AT MY DOOR?

B usy packing to move for a summer waitressing job, twenty-one-year-old Trish O'Leary was disrupted by knocking at her dormitory door on the second floor of Griggs Hall at Old Westbury College. Trish's gut reaction was not to answer the locked door; she didn't want to be distracted from leaving the campus as soon as possible. Remaining at the bucolic, private school on Long Island's North Shore felt lifeless. The spring semester of 1973 had ended and summer classes had not yet begun, so it was a time of lonely limbo on campus. Just a small number of students remained after graduation because they had no place else to go or were waiting to start summer sessions.

The Black Irish beauty with dark, southern European features from mixed ancestry was not expecting anyone, but believed the knocking may have come from her new boyfriend, a thirty-six-year-old married philosophy professor at the college. Dr. Lawrence Loewenstein was the type of professor whose classes everyone wanted to take; he was radical, compelling, and worshipped, and the good-looking professor was especially seductive to female students. While it was neither smart nor ethical for professors to mix privately with students, particularly in dormitory rooms, Trish believed his visit would be discreet and arousing. Breaking taboos excited her.

So, when the young coed heard knocking again, she turned the lock and opened her door slightly. In that instant, she realized her mistake. A stranger barged inside in the early afternoon, a time of day that made the intrusion even more brazen. Then the intruder locked the door, shutting out anyone who might have been on the second floor in the common area. In just minutes, the intruder forced Trish to swallow two quaaludes to sedate the girl so her arms and legs could easily be tied.

"What do you want?" Trish asked, with her speech a little slurred. "I don't have much money." The coed remained fully clothed, so apparently it was not about sex.

"I don't want your money or body. I just want to kill."

"Why?" she asked.

"I get satisfaction from killing, especially girls like you," her attacker bluntly replied.

"What have I done?" asked Trish, looking

perplexed.

The attacker looked straight into her eyes. "You've been acting like a whore. I've seen you with that older man. I've watched you being dropped off at the dormitory and going up to your room."

Then, their conversation ended. The stalker pulled a hunting knife from a sheath attached to their belt and made a left-handed cut across her throat. Moments later, Trish had been stabbed multiple times in her stomach, chest, and other areas of her body. Playing from a dormitory room across the hall was Roberta Flack's haunting musical refrain: *Killing me softly with his song...*

"Please, please stop," Trish begged. "You're a pig!" The music, melancholy in its lyrics and melody, drowned all hope of anyone hearing the girl's final cries.

"I'll stop when I'm tired," the killer retorted, incensed by her last words. Even after she was dead, the intruder's left arm continued the horror until it grew too heavy to thrust any longer.

T W O

DORMITORY BLUES

A black cloud hung over Long Island's North Shore campus throughout the summer of 1973, following Trish's brutal killing. When fall semester began, students wanted to get back to normalcy. One senior returning to Griggs Hall that September was Gavin Cole, who smelled and felt the crisp air transitioning from summer to autumn as he stepped from his flashy car. It was a 1966 bronze Corvair convertible that had a pancake engine in the back of the vehicle. With white racing stripes down the sides, the customized car featured black leather bucket seats, oversized wheels, a wooden steering wheel, and an AM/FM radio with a high-end sound system. It was a hot-looking car that turned heads, befitting its owner, who enjoyed the approval.

In the parking area in front of Griggs Hall, Cole stopped to admire his prized possession, then reached into the back seat to lift boxes of clothes and his stereo system and carried them to his familiar dormitory room. The near-autumn air made Gavin feel it was time to return to classes, as it had always been for him growing up and going back to school in September. He started thinking of fall's foliage soon appearing on campus, imagining leaves turning from brown to red, orange, and yellow and falling from the trees.

Despite feeling optimistic about the season, Cole could not shake the blues of returning to the scene where Trish was killed. Walking into his dormitory, considered experimental because it housed both men and women, he began reliving the events of that traumatic day. Gavin recalled packing boxes to move home for the summer when a campus maintenance man found him in a hallway on the ground floor and described what he saw: "It's bad," cried the campus worker, who had been ubiquitous around the grounds since Cole's freshman year. "She's lying on the floor of her room upstairs. I'm sure the girl is dead."

Remembering how his mouth turned dry, Cole also recalled his reply: "How do you know she's dead?"

The maintenance man had backed up his claim, as Cole recollected, in choppy statements: "Not moving. Blood all over her. Not responding to me. Could tell she stopped breathing."

Then Cole remembered going up to Trish's room, led by the maintenance man and campus carpenter. He could still visualize the bloody footprints on a gray carpet outside her room in the hall. "Be careful not to step in the footprints," Cole recalled saying to the carpenter. "You don't want to contaminate possible evidence." He had learned to avoid this misstep from watching crime scene investigations in film noir movies. Cole remembered peering through the half-open door and being stunned. Trish was lying in her room, her bound arms and legs clothed in a blood-stained yellow blouse and blue jeans. And he relived that dead silence, recalling the chilling mood inside her room.

Trying to break away from those bad images and thoughts, Cole began unpacking the boxes in his dormitory room to distract himself. Still, he could not erase the memory of Trish and how it all ended so deadly, with more than fifty Nassau County detectives swarming the campus from their mobile command post set up on the grounds.

Cole observed how the detectives questioned anyone they could find, all day and night, to uncover any clues to the crime. He thought about what was later reported in the media, that forensic detectives believed the killer was left-handed based on the angles of the knife wounds. Finally, Cole recalled how forensic detectives dusted the bloodied shoe prints with powdered brushes. He had heard how forensics could determine whether there was more than one killer at the crime scene as well as the sex of the killer; a wider and longer shoe print usually meant a man fled the crime scene.

The lead detective assigned to Trish's case, Homicide Detective Richard Rossi, learned that the campus carpenter was the first person to find Trish, so he initially questioned him on campus the day of the murder. Since Cole had been involved with the carpenter, he was there for the interview, which all came back to him.

"What time did you find her body in the room?" asked the detective.

"It was about three," the carpenter replied as he checked his watch.

"Did you see anyone unfamiliar or suspicious-looking hanging around the dormitory or anywhere on campus?" Rossi asked.

"From the back, I saw someone with long, dark hair and wearing jeans leaving Griggs Hall about a half hour before finding the girl in her room, but I couldn't tell if it was a man or woman."

In 1973, many young men and women wore their hair long and dressed in jeans, so from the back, it was not unusual for the carpenter to be unsure about the person's gender. Detective Rossi had to identify something more distinguishing.

Cole continued replaying Detective Rossi's interview with the carpenter: "Is there anything else that you remember?"

Cole recalled a long pause before the carpenter finally spoke, standing up from his seat in urgency. "Oh yes, the person was carrying something on their left shoulder. I couldn't see it clearly from a distance. That's all I know."

While the carpenter's interview was particularly important, there was still more work to be done. Interviewing as many students and campus workers as possible was key to learning more about the murder. Even the smallest clue could be a lead; nothing would be overlooked by Rossi, who was smart about putting clues together. During the early days of the investigation, learning the medical examiner's time of Trish's death was critical, because if that time closely matched the carpenter's claim about a someone leaving Griggs Hall around 2:30 p.m., the detective would have a suspect.

It had appeared Trish's killer slipped off campus, in daylight and out of sight. The killer may have inconspicuously left through the pine forest in the back of the campus, but only someone familiar with the campus would know about exiting that way.

During his summer vacation, Cole read in local newspapers that Trish's time of death was estimated at 2:13 p.m., which aligned with the time the carpenter said he saw someone leaving Griggs Hall. The seventeen-minute difference was just enough time for the killer to clean themself and remove any evidence from Trish's room.

The case, however, had gone cold. Even worse, the longer a cold case murder remains unresolved, the more difficult it is to solve.

THREE

THE RUSSIAN ACTING COACH AND MONTY

Preparing to start the 1973 fall semester, Cole realized it was time to turn the page on that dark day in June. His objective was to shake off those blues by studying in the Speech and Theater department while pursuing his dream of becoming a professional actor.

One of Cole's classes was an upper-level acting course, which was taught by a renowned lady of the stage and screen. She was Marina Rostova, a Russian-born drama coach who arrived on campus as a visiting professor for that fall semester. Students who knew Rostova's background were awed by her.

At sixty-five years old, her prematurely white hair was cut short, framing her China doll face and blue eyes. Despite Rostova's white hair, which added to her aura, she had been aging well, applying little makeup to her porcelain skin. Her modest clothes were emblematic of her Russian roots. She was all about substance over style.

To enter Professor Rostova's class, students had to audition. It suggested that she wanted to work only with gifted actors who understood her style of method acting. Therefore, pre-semester auditions were underway at the college's Little Theater. It was a wood-framed building with limited seating that had opened with the school in 1954.

As part of Cole's preparation for his audition, he believed it would be beneficial to research Professor Rostova's history. His thinking was that it might help him to be more comfortable auditioning for her.

Cole discovered Rostova left Russia with her family after the 1917 revolution, changed her name from Rosovskaya, and began her acting career in Austria and Germany. He also learned the Stanislavs-ki-trained actress came to America in the late 1930s; she met Hollywood great Montgomery Clift when she starred with him in an experimental play on Broadway in 1942. Cole was surprised to learn that Rostova quit her promising stage career early, without explanation, to become Clift's exclusive acting coach.

Famous for his emotional depth and vulnerability on screen, Monty, as he was known among close friends, was the forerunner of Marlon Brando and James Dean. The three Hollywood stars made up an iconic trinity of method actors, but Monty was the first American method actor who became both critically acclaimed and a Hollywood star. The actor's success was largely rooted in his Russian drama coach, who was a master at her own method-style acting and devoted to Monty.

Moreover, Cole was fascinated to learn about Rostova's actions on a movie set with the actor. She accompanied him on set and closely studied his work. She either nodded with approval or shook her head in disapproval, while trying to stay invisible behind set pieces. Some directors despised Rostova's on-set presence, seeing it as a distraction. In Clift's 1959 film, *Wild River*, with the lovely Lee Remick, director Elia Kazan kicked Rostova off the set despite her talent. The brilliant director Alfred Hitchcock hated her meddling, as he could not click with Clift while filming 1953's *I Confess*. In a clash of egos between Hitchcock and Rostova, the director believed Rostova got between himself and Monty.

However, despite some directors' disdain for Rostova, Cole was impressed by her history and especially admired her legacy coaching Clift, who became legendary. Cole could hardly wait to audition for the charismatic acting coach.

The night before auditioning, Cole rehearsed his monologue from Arthur Miller's *Death of a Salesman* one last time. He felt comfortable with his overall preparation, but anticipating his audition made sleeping difficult.

The next morning, the student actors, all of whom were buzzing about their preparation, entered the Little

Theater. Professor Rostova, who had to quiet them down, explained her auditioning process. "Prior to your audition, please introduce yourself to everyone in the audience, tell us the scene you chose, and explain your reason for selecting the scene." After looking at her roster of students, Rostova glanced up to scan the group. "Mr. Cole, can you please start the auditions?"

Cole nervously walked to the stage, and he looked at Professor Rostova and his peers. A single spotlight was on him. "I'm Gavin Cole. I'm a senior majoring in Speech and Theater. I'd like to perform a monologue delivered by Biff in a scene from Arthur Miller's *Death of a Salesman*. I chose this monologue because I identify with the character's vulnerability. He's conflicted over yearning for a future while fearing that he's wasting his life."

During his audition, Cole diverted his eyes away from the acting coach to avoid feeling nervous, as he found her gaze and intensity intimidating.

He reminds me of Monty, Rostova thought, as she evaluated Cole's audition and made notes.

After auditions were completed, Rostova addressed the students. "Thank you all for your preparation and auditions. You soon will be notified by the department about being accepted in my class." Cole would anxiously await the professor's decision, which he believed could positively impact his acting career. He was excited about studying with a coach who guided the great Montgomery Clift to stardom, thinking she could be a pathway to his acting success, too.

FOUR

INTO THE WEEDS: GIBBY WITH HIS GUITAR

Cole had been trying to put the murder of Trish O'Leary behind him. He had been accepted in Marina Rostova's class, and he was moving on with acting and enjoying campus life, but there were times when he still envisioned Trish's pretty face and long legs in her denim jeans. Imagining her while crossing the campus's Great Lawn to the professor's acting class triggered his thinking to a drifter who showed up on campus in late January 1973. It was about five months prior to Trish's killing, and because Cole wondered about this drifter's possible connection to her, he retraced what had happened. It had all started in Florida.

During the winter break in early January 1973, Cole and a dorm buddy from his freshman year hitch-hiked to Miami Beach. When they arrived there at night, they were unable to get a room. Everything was booked, as it was high season for college students looking to escape the pressure of their studies. The hitchhikers discovered an obscure area of tall weeds, where they camped for the night and dropped LSD, which had remained popular on college campuses since the early 1960s. Soon, the acid trip built in euphoric waves, heightening the intoxicating scent of Florida's Angel's Trumpet and Jimsonweed flowers. At its peak, they looked up to see a very tall character, about six-foot-four, standing over them. They were not hallucinating. He had long, reddish-brown hair and a thick mustache with pale, freckled skin and a droopy, dead left eye. Despite experiencing visual distortion from their acid trip, the dormmates clearly saw a guitar slung over the man's back. He had the persona of singer-songwriter troubadours from the early 1970s.

"I'm Gibby Carson. I see you found my hideaway in the weeds." The guitar man sat on the ground with both boys. "I adopted my first name from my acoustic Gibson guitar," he said as he pointed to the instrument on his back. "The name has stuck with me wherever I go. I go to a lot of places around the country. If I like it there, I stay a while, and when I'm tired of the place, I move on wherever the wind blows me."

Mesmerized by Gibby's magnetism, the college friends watched him pull a large marijuana joint from the front pocket of his dirty jeans. He lit up, took a long hit, and gave it to Cole, who took a puff and passed it to his buddy.

"How did you end up in these weeds?" asked the drifter.

"After hitchhiking here from our college on Long Island's North Shore, we couldn't get a room," Cole replied, as Gibby took a mental note.

"Can I play my guitar for you boys?" Gibby asked.

"We'd like that," said Cole, knowing Gibby's guitar playing would enhance their psychedelic trip. He noticed the musician played guitar with his left hand, an uncommon trait. Gibby's music struck a chord and bonded the three men until his playing and singing caused the two boys to nod off in semi-consciousness. At daybreak, when Cole and his friend awoke after coming down from their trip, the troubadour was gone.

Three Weeks Later

Shortly after returning to school for 1973's spring semester, Cole was shocked to see Gibby turn up on campus. *Look what the wind blew in*, he thought, remembering the drifter's words. "How the hell did you find this campus and get here?" asked Cole, looking at that same Gibson on Gibby's back.

"Well, you said you came from a college on Long Island's North Shore. There are limited college campuses in this area. And I hitchhiked, of course."

Soon, Gibby ingratiated himself among the students on campus with his guitar and big personality. Using his charm, he became part of the campus fabric, even taking a job playing and singing on Wednesday and Saturday nights in the Rathskeller, a popular meeting place where students gathered to drink beer, socialize, and be entertained.

In the early 1970s, lax security was common on the campus, and strangers like Gibby could easily enter the grounds and stay there. These campus crashers either sat in on classes, worked at college jobs, or merely played. There were characters like Johnny B, who was tall and lanky, with his puffed, curly blond hair and the tie-dyed T-shirts he created. Then there was Roger Boylen, with his beautiful, chiseled looks and straight, shoulder-length dark brown hair. He wore scuffed combat boots, had a hoop in his right ear, and smelled of Patchouli and sex. The man walked on campus like he was the second coming of Jesus, and young college women flocked to him.

Johnny B and Roger were members of a tight-knit, colorful campus group that reminded Cole of American author Ken Kesey's Merry Pranksters. The band of jokers were Kesey's followers, all of whom fueled the LSD '60s with their *Magic Trip* bus documentary across America. Gibby, given his large and unusual personality, easily would have fit in with the Merry Prankster-like campus group if their paths had crossed. Cole sometimes socialized with the group's members because he was curious about life's wild side.

Once, the young actor participated in a stoned-out night seeing rock's Jefferson Airplane at the iconic

Fillmore East in the East Village. That night, the Airplane played one of their longest shows, performing encore after encore until the lights came up. After Cole and the campus group finally left the theater, they went to a pot-smoking party in a West Village brownstone apartment. There, through the doorway of a bedroom, Cole saw and heard sounds of group sex for the first time.

Gibby and Trish

Several months after the drifter suddenly left the campus grounds in the spring of '73, Cole recalled Gibby's association with Trish. She had served beer in the Rathskeller, where Gibby had performed. *Perhaps she and Gibby were even friendly*, Gavin thought. Certainly, Gibby knew how to take advantage of women and had every opportunity. At one point, he even shared a dormitory room with a young woman who had not been assigned a roommate.

Gibby was a con man who fooled her and everyone on campus. Eventually, he blew his cover as the big nice guy. It was only a matter of time, after record albums and jewelry were discovered missing from the dormitory rooms of several students who did not lock their doors. Unlocked doors were part of the liberal environment on campus. The valuables were found under a bed in the room where Gibby had been sleeping with his duped girlfriend. When the con man was confronted by Cole and his dormmates about the stolen property, the drifter took off—once again.

After Cole looked back at Gibby's time on campus, he felt morally obligated that fall to report the events involving the vagabond's stay there. *Was it possible Gibby had slipped back on campus the day Trish was murdered?* he questioned himself. That thought caused him to visit Detective Rossi, adding what he knew to the investigation. But it seemed too late, as the elusive traveler could have moved anywhere in the country.

FIVE

TEACHER'S PET

Cole focused his attention on acting at a new level during the fall semester. He learned about becoming a character by drawing on past emotional experiences, using sensory techniques, and telling the truth. Marina Rostova taught the process through her personal Method style—the same way she had trained Monty.

Cole began complementing this training by working on his stage presence. Professor Lillian Lampton, who taught Cole's Speech Arts class, showed students how to use their instrument effectively to develop presence. The professor had turned to teaching after growing older and putting her Broadway fame behind her. Tall and lean, she kept her ash-blond hair long, and she had a style that Rostova lacked. Cole especially liked Lampton's style combined with her sophistication.

Juggling both Professor Lampton's and Rostova's classes, Cole was gaining confidence as an actor. Further building his ego, he sensed that Professor Lampton seemed smitten with him. Cole saw her furtive glances when he entered class. It was psychology textbook attraction: the divorced, mid-fiftyish woman who maintained her allure by carrying herself like she was still theater royalty was drawn to her much younger, attractive student.

Cole soon learned from Little Theater gossip that Lampton knew Rostova from the New York stage and the ladies associated with mutual friends from theater circles and had frequented the same Manhattan parties and restaurants. The speech professor had even persuaded Rostova to teach at the college during that fall semester.

In addition to teaching speech classes, Professor Lampton had been negotiating with her department to direct a theater production that she could take on the road to Pittsburgh, Pennsylvania; Worcester, Massachusetts; and Wooster, Ohio.

Professor Lampton convinced Cole to stay after class one day to discuss an opportunity to join the cast. "I'd like to offer you a role as the narrator in a stage production that I'll be directing. You don't need to audition because I believe you're perfect for this part— and you will be working with professional actors, whom I'm casting from my circle of stage friends. I promise they will be generous, and you will learn more from this experience than any acting class."

Cole was slow to react, as he felt uneasy about

leaping from working with student actors to professionals. Then, he thought about how the experience might make him a better actor. "Alright," Cole replied, "I'll join the cast since you have confidence in me, and I'm looking forward to working under your direction."

Cast of Characters

The Renaissance play was entitled *The Borgias: Deadly Sins*. It was about a powerful fifteenth and sixteenth century Vatican family that provoked scandalous rumors, including incest, and suffered a brother's murder.

Showing up for the first-night script reading were Marina Rostova, whom Professor Lampton invited to rehearsals to especially coach Cole; Dianna Perrill, a willowy, cool blond socialite-actress connected to the campus through her very rich family that sold their estate's land and properties to the college—Griggs Hall, in fact, was named after Dianna's half-sister; Wes Addison, a Broadway, film, and television character actor; and Addison's actress-wife Celestine Houseman, who once starred with Sinatra, Crosby, Peck, and other Hollywood legends. The acting couple was very close friends with Professor Lampton, who had performed on Broadway with both actors. Another cast member, whose experience with the cast took a surprising turn, was Henry Heaton. The actor, who was bearded, handsome, and well-groomed, lived in Glen Cove, Long

Island, where he was known for acting in community theater. Because his stage career had slowed, Professor Lampton, who knew him from parties hosted by celebrity columnist Dotti Killian, wanted to give him work. New to the group was Gavin Cole, theater student and aspiring actor who had been recruited by his professor.

Already cast in their roles, the actors sat around a long, rectangular table and formally introduced themselves. Then they read the script, with each actor taking their part, to get a feel for their characterization and the relationships among characters. During the reading, Cole saw Heaton glance at him, which was the impetus for both actors running lines together outside rehearsals.

SIX

LUNCH AT GLEN COVE: FOOD FOR THOUGHT

The day after the first-night reading, Cole went to Heaton's cottage to have lunch and run lines. Heaton's Glen Cove home was located on Landing Road, just off Germaine Street. It was a scenic location, with Landing Road being a dead-end block overlooking Hempstead Bay.

Walking past a garden and up the stone stairs, Cole and Heaton entered the home through the front door. Once inside, Cole was astonished by what he saw: photographs of Montgomery Clift were displayed throughout Heaton's rooms like a shrine to the dead actor. There were candid shots of Monty on beaches of Long Island's South Shore; eight-by-ten black-and-white professional photos of the legendary actor; pictures of the two men together, some with Clift's arm around Heaton's shoulder; and other pictures of the former star in dramatic poses.

Monty and Me

"How did you know Montgomery Clift?" asked Cole.

"I knew him well," replied Heaton, laughingly.

"I meant how did you meet him? But since you mentioned it, how well did you know him?"

Heaton paused to think about a smooth reply. "As well as you can know someone."

Cole was perceptive enough to understand Heaton's meaning, but he needed to be clear. "Do you mean you were more than just friends?"

"Yes. We were in an on-and-off-again relationship from the early '50s until he died in 1966."

"So how did you meet?"

Heaton was preparing lunch in the kitchen but paused to look at Cole. "I met Monty at one of Dotti Killian's famous townhouse parties on the Upper East Side. Dotti was a nationally-syndicated, celebrity columnist who knew many high-profile people from Broadway to Hollywood and Washington, D.C. That night, Joan Crawford and Marilyn Monroe, Killian's close friends, were there. In fact, I saw Marilyn eyeing Monty. I overheard her whispering to Dotti, 'Can you introduce me to Monty? He's so sexy.'" Heaton grinned wryly about that moment.

"Those parties generally lasted until four in the

morning," noted Heaton. "That night, when the party ended, Monty, Dianna Perrill, and I left together. We went to breakfast at the Brasserie, a well-known restaurant on East Fifty-Third Street between Lexington and Park, near Killian's townhouse. After partying, people went there to continue talking until the sun came up."

The two actors sat at a table for lunch, but as they were about to eat, they heard knocking at the side door to the kitchen. Tentatively, Heaton got up to answer. When he opened the door, Cole noticed a burly man standing there. He watched the men whisper to each other, then Henry elbowed the big man away.

Heaton sat to continue his lunch with Gavin and telling more stories, but the young actor was curious about the incident.

"Who was that at the door?" Cole asked.

"Oh, don't be concerned about him. He's just another actor I know."

Cole brushed off the incident, but he felt something was odd.

Despite the distraction, the twosome enjoyed their tuna salad with bottles of Perrier. Cole, still curious, wanted to learn more about Clift and Heaton. "What happened after that first meeting with Monty?"

"Monty and I became close. I used to help him run lines for his movies, whenever he wasn't getting coached by Marina Rostova. He adored Marina. He even had a fling with her in the early days, though she was older and motherly to him. After we got to know each other better, Monty started staying over at my place. We had breakfast together, exactly where we are sitting now. Monty was beautiful, until he crashed his car in '56. He never was the same after the accident."

Cole knew of Monty's accident, but he only knew what had been rumored. "Tell me more about the accident," requested Cole, who was engaged in lunch and the conversation, nearly forgetting about running lines for Professor Lampton's stage production.

"Monty was filming *Raintree County* with Elizabeth Taylor when a break from location led to the accident. He was driving home from a house party at Liz's place in the Hollywood Hills when he fell asleep at the wheel and smacked his car into a telephone pole. Luckily, Monty's good friend, actor Kevin McCarthy, was driving behind him after leaving the party and witnessed the accident. So, Kevin returned to Liz's party to alert her about the crash. When she arrived at the scene, she broke a car window to open the door and found Monty in bad shape. His face was bloodied and damaged, and he was choking. Liz reached into his throat and pulled out both front teeth."

After learning the details of Clift's car accident, Cole was able to better understand the aftermath. He had read that reconstructive surgery helped put Clift's face together, but the leading man had lost his sculptured good looks. Thus, at the peak of Monty's movie career, the accident caused his downward spiral—even into alcoholism and drugs that he used for the pain. His acting remained superb in films that followed the crash, but he was no longer leading-man handsome; he took character roles.

Over coffee that followed their lunch, Cole wondered how actress Dianna Perrill had fit into Clift's and Heaton's lives, especially because he noticed the vibe between her and Heaton during the reading. "I noticed that Dianna and you still seem connected, but can you explain Monty's relationship with the both of you?" asked Gavin.

"Where should I start?" Henry paused to think about something dramatic. "I'll tell you about our skinny dipping. Dianna invited Monty and me to tour her family estate, after we met at Dotti Killian's party but before your college purchased the estate. You may know that she's the heiress to her family's cereal fortune, and your college purchased the land and buildings for its campus."

Gavin knew some of the college's history, but he naturally was more intrigued about the skinny dipping.

"Dianna took us to the stables, where she kept her horse. She showed us the pine forest, where she said that she would lie on the pine needles and dream of becoming an actress. Then we went inside that life-size dollhouse her family built for her and where she played as a young girl. You know it, of course. The one standing between Griggs Hall and the indoor swimming pool. We entered the pool area after midnight. She had the keys to get inside after hours. Well, we enjoyed a night swim, skinny dipping."

Cole identified with the night swim and laughed with a smirk. "I've done some skinny dipping there, too. We'd sneak in late through one of the broken plexiglass panes that enclose the pool. It was the sneaking in that made it exciting." Heaton laughed along with Cole.

Poignantly, Henry finished his story. "Putting all our playing aside, I know Dianna loved Monty as much as I did."

The mood turned heartfelt as the two actors quietly finished their coffee. Finally, they ran through their lines for Professor Lampton's production about the Vatican's Borgia family and the five-hundred-year-old cold case murder of the pope's son.

SEVEN

STAGING A COLD CASE MURDER

When the cast of Professor Lampton's production met at the college's Little Theater to start rehearsals the next day, the professor set up the scene for rehearsal.

"We'll begin at the opening of Act I, Scene 1, when Rodrigo Borgia, Pope Alexander VI, discovers his favorite son, Juan, is missing. The scene begins with the pope and his other three children, Cesare, Lucrezia, and Jofre, gathering in a room at the Vatican to discuss what they might have known about Juan's disappearance on the evening of June 14, 1497."

The actors in the scene took their places on stage.

Pope Alexander (Wes Addison), speaking to three of his children: *Juan has not returned from your mother's dinner party. It's now been one full day. I know he has a habit of walking the streets of Rome at night, but I'm worried over his whereabouts. Do any of you know where he was going when he left the party?*

Lucrezia (Dianna Perrill): *All I know is that Juan sent his companions, including our brother, Cesare, away on some mysterious errand. I understood that Juan was meeting a woman.*

Pope Alexander, addressing his children: *Gather all my men and send them into the streets of Rome to search for Juan.*

Professor Lampton turned to Wes Addison. "Juan is the pope's favorite son. If Juan were your own son, how would you feel?"

Addison had a gut reaction. "Panicked."

"You must deeply feel this emotion," she directed. "Find it with something you've experienced in your life and let it bubble up inside you. Then, your words will be truthful. Now, let's continue with the scene."

Narrator (Gavin Cole), standing at a podium downstage left; minimal scenery suggests that the narrator is an external observer: *After an exhausting search through Rome, one eyewitness was found two days after Juan's disappearance. This witness, a timber merchant watching for a nighttime lumber shipment on the Tiber River, said he saw something horrible. The witness described someone riding a white horse with a body hanging over the saddle. Then, the rider stopped and ordered four men trailing behind on foot to dump the body into the river. The merchant noted that he continued to watch as the men carried out the order and threw stones on the body to sink it. After watching the body slowly submerge, he said all the men entered a narrow alley and disappeared into the night.*

Professor Lampton continued her direction. "Gavin, your overall presence is drawing attention to you. That's good! Your interpretation of the narrative and body language make your delivery compelling. Your audience will naturally be engaged by the intrigue of murder and graphic actions, but you must reach everyone at the back of the theater. Your projection is trailing off with a longer narration like this one. Remember what we worked on in class. You need to stop for a dramatic pause, where that works in the script, and take in air. This will emphasize the drama as well as sustain your breath control for a stronger projection. Now, let's continue with the first act's next scene."

Cesare (Henry Heaton) enters from a garden within the walls of the Vatican and approaches Pope Alexander, who enters from the opposite side: *I've got very sad news, father. A timber merchant watching for shipments on the Tiber River saw a body dumped into the river the night Juan went missing. They pulled the body from the river today—and it was Juan. He was stabbed to death.*

Pope Alexander: *How does he look?*
Cesare: *You don't want to know those details.*
Pope Alexander: *Tell me!*
Cesare: *He had nine stab wounds across his body.*
Pope Alexander: *Was his face cut?*

Cesare: *Yes.*

Pope Alexander: *Make sure his face is fixed. I don't want the people of Rome seeing him that way.*

Cesare: *I'll handle it, father. You should know he still had thirty ducats in a purse attached to his belt, so it wasn't robbery.*

Pope Alexander: *Then, we must make inquiries and find the motive. Once we learn the motive, it will lead us to who ordered Juan's assassination.*

Professor Lampton liked what she saw. "That was excellent, as neither of you missed a beat. The pacing was perfect. I can tell that you really listened to each other and reacted. That's essential to acting. Everyone in the cast should understand the importance of listening."

And that concluded the first rehearsal. Professor Lampton spoke to the cast about the rehearsal schedule going forward, and then everyone except Rostova and Lampton went their separate ways. Together, they side-eyed Henry and Gavin pairing off while leaving the theater. "I wonder what's going on between those two," Lampton whispered to Rostova.

As the two men exited the theater, they made plans to go for a drive around Glen Cove the next day, since Cole did not have afternoon classes on Tuesdays.

EIGHT

REVELATION AT
THE DOLLHOUSE

Tuesday afternoon, Cole felt good about being free from classes while looking forward to getting to know Henry better. Cole got into his Corvair, which was parked opposite Griggs Hall, and turned on the ignition. He put the canvas top down, as mid-October's Indian summer day was perfect for driving in a convertible. Exiting the campus, Gavin made a right turn on Northern Boulevard, heading to Glen Cove. He remembered the directions and found Heaton's home easily.

"I'll be with you in a few minutes," said Henry when he answered the door. "I just want to close the bedroom window." While Gavin waited, he looked once again at Monty's pictures. The photos reminded him there was more to learn about Henry's relationship with the Hollywood star. "My window locks are broken," called Henry from his bedroom. "I'll have to fix them soon—but it's generally safe in this neighborhood."

Anxious to cruise Glenn Cove, the castmates left and hit the road. Heaton was impressed with Cole's car. "Great looking car!" he remarked. "Where did you find it?"

Before replying, Cole turned on the FM radio. "You'll like the sound system, too. I bought it from a car lover who restored cars in my old Brooklyn neighborhood back in '68. He customized the car, and I was obsessed at first sight."

Listening to Led Zeppelin, Elton John, the Allman Brothers Band, and other recording artists of the time, the actors talked about music and movies while driving through Glen Cove. "Have you seen *Midnight Cowboy*?" asked Heaton.

"No, but I heard the movie was controversial for its time when it came out."

Heaton paused, feeling emotional about the film. "The compassion between the two characters played by Jon Voight and Dustin Hoffman, combined with that moving soundtrack, hit me hard," he said.

When Heaton grew quiet, Cole thought, *I'm sure he's thinking about Monty.* Clift didn't come up in conversation, but it seemed Cole knew just what Heaton was thinking, and words that might have been said between them weren't needed.

"Anyway, I think you should see the movie," persuaded Heaton. "I can't explain something that must be felt."

Then a familiar, melancholy refrain aired over the radio: *Killing me softly with his song...* and Gavin began thinking of Trish. "You probably heard about that young girl who was murdered on my campus last June."

"Actually, I was on campus the day she was killed."

Distracted by Heaton's statement, Cole gripped the steering wheel with renewed concentration. "That's a coincidence!" he said, focusing on the cars in front of him. "Why were you on campus that day?"

"I heard around theater circles Marina was interviewing on campus for a teaching position at the college. I had gotten to know her, of course, through Monty. We hadn't spoken since his funeral service, but I still had her number, so I called her to suggest meeting on campus that day and having lunch in Glen Cove. And she agreed."

"Is that it?" asked Gavin, stopping at a red light and turning to Henry.

"No, there's more. A lot more. After parking my car close to Griggs Hall, I started walking to the theater where Marina was interviewing. I was feeling really nostalgic as I passed Dianna's old dollhouse. It looked the same as when she first invited Monty and me to her family's estate."

"I know you stopped to look through the window to see if everything remained the same on the inside, too. Right?"

Henry smiled mischievously. "Yes, but when I did, I saw a tall, nervous-looking woman through the opposite window, rushing out of Griggs Hall. As this woman got closer, I noticed she was wearing tinted glasses and turning her head from side to side, looking all around and acting fidgety. She had long brown hair that was a little greasy. I remember her wearing bell-bottom jeans and a silky blouse, with a long scarf around her neck that covered her chest."

Cole pulled over to park and digest everything Heaton had told him. "That seems so suspicious to me," said the young actor. "Why didn't you come forward with this information earlier? The detective investigating Trish's murder would have wanted to know about it."

"You're probably right," replied Henry. "When the woman got closer to the dollhouse, I studied her face. At the same time, she stopped for a moment and noticed me standing behind the dollhouse. We locked eyes. She looked attractive, with dangling earrings and glossy lips, but something looked off about her. When the woman passed, I turned to watch her from the back. She walked quickly but awkwardly toward the indoor swimming pool, then disappeared on the other side of the building. Oh, I forgot! She was carrying a bag over her left shoulder."

Maybe the woman was heading to the pine forest to get off campus from the back end, Cole thought. "You saw a lot. Do you remember the time?"

Henry paused to retrace his steps before answering. "Yes, it was sometime between two and two-thirty because I was about to meet Marina at two forty-five."

The approximate time resonated with Cole because it was during the time frame when the campus carpenter spotted someone leaving the dormitory. However, the carpenter did not say the person was wearing bell-bottoms. Cole believed the carpenter was not as observant as Henry, so chances are they witnessed the same person.

"You must tell your story to the Nassau County detective in charge of investigating Trish's murder," Cole recommended emphatically.

"Will you go with me tomorrow, if you're free from classes?"

"I have afternoon class with Professor Rostova, but we can visit Detective Rossi in the early morning. We'll have to schedule a meeting with him to be sure he's around to see us."

Gavin then drove Henry to his front garden. "I'll check with Rossi, and will let you know if he's available to meet in the morning," Gavin said as he opened the car door for Henry.

Hoping his revelation might make a difference, Heaton nodded to Cole in approval. Then he turned to walk up the stone stairway to his front door.

"Remember to fix those window locks!" Cole shouted.

The Glen Cove actor turned to gesture a thumbs-up.

The Next Day: Something Doesn't Fit

After arranging an early morning meeting with Detective Rossi, Cole picked up Heaton and drove to Old Westbury's police station, a 1924 ranch-style brick building next to the courthouse, town hall, and post office. The row of buildings with trees and shrubbery facing them suggested a small-town atmosphere that belied Trish's gruesome murder. As the two actors passed the flagpole near the station house, they paused to read an epitaph on a monument dedicated to deceased members of the Old Westbury Police Department.

Heaton and Cole entered the station and approached the desk sergeant who was on the phone behind a glass window. While they waited, a *Times-Journal* reporter was standing around looking for any news his paper could publish.

The reporter appeared to recognize Heaton and buttonholed the actors. "I know you," he said, eyeing Henry. "You're that actor."

Like most actors, Heaton enjoyed being recognized. "Well, I am an actor, but how do you know me?"

"You're Henry Heaton," noted the reporter. "I've seen you in local stage shows. What are you doing now?"

Before Heaton could answer, the conversation shifted. "What can I do for you?" asked the sergeant, addressing the two actors.

"We have an appointment with Detective Rossi

about Trish O'Leary's murder," replied Heaton, as the reporter leaned in to listen. "I have new evidence to discuss with him."

Checking his schedule, the sergeant confirmed Heaton and Cole were on it and called Rossi to let him know they were at the front desk.

"Okay, send them to my office," said Rossi.

"We need a break on the O'Leary case," the sergeant said in a lowered voice to avoid being overheard. "We're feeling some heat about it from the top."

Heaton knocked on the detective's door, feeling nervous about telling his story for the official record, and he knew he would be grilled by Rossi. Plus, if the person Heaton saw on campus was caught, charged, and put on trial, the actor would be summoned to testify in court.

Detective Rossi opened the door to his office, and the actors studied the pictures and sketches of crime suspects on the wall behind the detective's desk. They were suspects still on the loose, but there was nothing of Trish's killer, since the murder remained a cold case. While the actors sat close to the detective's desk, they could see the wood had scars from age. The nicks, scratches, and scuff marks seemingly represented Rossi's psychological scars from horrific murder investigations.

Rossi remembered Cole from the on-campus investigation of the coed killing. After Heaton introduced himself, the actor revealed he had new information about

Trish O'Leary's murder. Heaton, naturally observant as an experienced actor, studied the detective. He watched him unfasten two buttons of his tweed sports jacket, which showed a holster strapped to his right shoulder. Then, Rossi asked Heaton for permission to record his statement, to which he agreed.

First, Henry set the stage. He explained he was on campus the day Trish was murdered to meet Marina Rostova, who, he said, was interviewing for a faculty position in the theater department. Then the actor described the woman he encountered at the dollhouse on that deadly day.

"Did you notice if this woman was wearing a higher heel?" The detective wondered if the woman's shoe could have matched the large, wide footprint outside Trish's dormitory room. *That footprint seemed too large and wide to be a woman's*, he thought. *Something doesn't fit.*

Heaton tried to create a mental picture. "Not that I recall."

"How tall was she?" asked Rossi.

"I cannot say exactly, but she appeared very tall for a woman."

"When you crossed paths with her at the dollhouse, what was your gut reaction?"

That question hit home with Heaton. "She was flamboyant, and I felt this negative energy. Maybe it was her nervous body language that made me feel uneasy."

Heaton's reference to "flamboyant" struck a

nerve with Rossi, but the detective kept his thoughts to himself. "Is there anything else that stood out?" he asked. "Think hard, because even the smallest detail could mean something."

The tinted glasses that she wore stood out, thought Henry. "You know, she might have been hiding something from behind the tinted glasses I mentioned."

Listening to the exchange, Cole thought someone may have passed the dollhouse while hiding in plain sight. *What about Gibby and his droopy, dead eye?* the young actor questioned himself. *That eye was something he might want to hide at times, but could there be a feminine side to Gibby?* Cole squashed that last outrageous thought and never discussed it.

Though Detective Rossi's meeting with Henry shed new light on the O'Leary case, nothing had been definitively determined. It still was a cold case.

Dogging the Detective

When the two actors left Rossi's office, the *Times-Journal* reporter was still hanging around. He sought after the detective to see what the meeting had produced, but Rossi made it clear to the journalist that he had police business and couldn't take time to talk.

So, the reporter switched to Plan B, which was to seek out the detective at a steak house in Old Brookville, where judges, court officers, attorneys, and cops congregated after work. The reporter knew Rossi liked going to the restaurant and bar. *He just might be there later*, the journalist thought on a hunch.

Driving to his destination, the reporter was thinking about how to get Detective Rossi to talk. He arrived at the steak house around twilight and parked in a lot out front. As he got close to the restaurant's heavy, wide wooden doors, the smell of steak permeated outside. The *Times-Journal* reporter opened the doors and walked past crowded tables, hearing but not listening to lots of cross-talk. Just as he had hunched, Detective Rossi was at the bar drinking shots. *A couple of more and Rossi likely will loosen up*, the reporter thought as he moved closer. *He won't be so guarded.*

"Can I buy you a drink?" the journalist asked Rossi, sneaking up behind him.

"You're like gum under my shoe!" joked the detective.

"That's funny, you know…gumshoe detective," the journalist quipped.

"Clever comeback. Sure, I'll have another scotch. Johnnie Walker neat."

The reporter ordered the same for himself but with ice. He wanted to be in control.

"Okay, what's your angle?" asked Rossi.

"No angle. I'm just doing my job."

After another round of drinks and some small talk, the reporter saw Rossi was mellowing. *Now is the time to get serious*, he thought. "You know it's my job to stay on top of the O'Leary case," said the reporter. "I heard that actor, Heaton, mention Trish O'Leary to the desk sergeant earlier. So, what did Heaton tell you?"

The detective paused to gather his thoughts before answering. "He told me about a woman he saw passing that dollhouse at Old Westbury's campus, shortly after the O'Leary girl was murdered."

The reporter recognized the woman was news. "Who was she?"

Rossi, reluctant to say too much, would only summarize a description. "First, we don't know her name. But she is tall for a woman. And she wore bell-bottom jeans and tinted glasses and had a shoulder bag."

The reporter, who had been covering the story since Trish's murder, was conflicted. Like Rossi, he thought the woman seen by Heaton didn't match the initial impression of Trish's killer. "I'm curious about that shoulder bag," he said. "Did she wear it over her right or left shoulder? Perhaps your observation might indicate whether she's left- or right-handed. And we all know, as it's been established, that Trish's killer is left-handed."

"She wore the bag over her left shoulder," revealed Rossi as he demonstrated his actions, "so that suggests to me she's left-handed." He reached toward his left side with his right hand. "If she needed to get something from her bag, she naturally would cross over with her right hand to hold the bag and use her left hand to reach into it. Do you see what I mean?"

NINE

1967: THE PLANTING FIELDS KILLINGS

Following drinking and talking with the *Times-Journal* reporter, Detective Rossi drove home, half sober, to his one-bedroom apartment, where he moved after his wife left him when she could no longer live with a homicide detective's dark side. He found his place in colonial-rooted Oyster Bay, named for its scenic harbor on Long Island's North Shore.

It had been another long day for the detective, and he just wanted to sleep, but the Trish O'Leary case kept him awake once again. He got up and walked to the liquor cabinet to pour a shot of Courvoisier. The French brandy always helped him sleep.

He slept until a recurring dream awakened him between two and three a.m. The detective screamed as he jumped from his sleep, but his scream was not triggered by the image of Trish O'Leary's dead body, with her slit neck and clothes bloodied from multiple cuts and stab wounds. Rather, his nightmare resulted from scars left by investigating the Planting Fields killings of 1967, six years earlier. Pictures he saw in his sleep presented victims' heads sticking up from the ground of the Planting Fields.

The historic state park, in the village of Upper Brookville in the town of Oyster Bay, attracted college acid heads who tripped on LSD to heighten the park's beauty. The sprawling Gold Coast estate had everything: a hallucinator's dream of art, architecture, and landscape. The grounds featured over four hundred acres of greenhouses, rolling lawns, formal gardens, woodland paths, and amazing plant collections.

However, the Planting Fields also attracted a serial killer who preyed on victims in their most vulnerable, drug-induced state, especially along the woodland paths. The victims, lost in their hallucinations, were oblivious to the stalker's preying eyes. But once the psychopath struck from behind with a hammer, his victims' euphoria suddenly became a bad trip. All his prey—single men and women and couples—had their heads smashed, resulting in a painful death. Then, the serial killer buried their bodies feet first, with only their heads sticking out of the ground like heads of cabbage in a cabbage patch. That was his signature.

After a one-year manhunt, that serial murderer, dubbed the Hammerhead Killer by the New York media, was caught. Detective Rossi, who orchestrated a dangerous trap, was credited with his capture.

No Rest for the Weary

Unable to fall back asleep, the detective replayed the cat-and-mouse trap in his head: A young male and female undercover cop, posing as a couple, set their trap at one of the Planting Fields' woodland paths. Pretending to be dropping LSD every day for a week, they baited the Hammerhead Killer and waited for him to strike. Meanwhile, Nassau County police helicopters circled high above, out of sight from anyone involved in the sting on the ground but ready to swoop down on their target.

Finally, Rossi dozed, and the Hammerhead Killer's capture concluded in his recurring dream: The undercover couple were sitting on a bench making out in the woodlands. Appearing as lovers, they seemed oblivious to what was happening around them, but the undercover cops were keenly aware. Theirs was a game of chicken. The killer had to be very close and caught in the act of attacking them, or an arrest would not stick. In his dream, Detective Rossi saw several police helicopters circling high in the sky with pilots who were waiting to be radioed in to quicky descend on the suspect. During his distorted dream, the detective saw *bumblebees* buzzing in the sky; a professional analyzing dreams may believe Rossi associated bees with a sting operation.

Awakened once again, Detective Rossi's nightmare

lingered with him. This time, he went to the kitchen for coffee instead of going back to sleep. As the coffee was brewing, he recalled how it all ended that day the Hammerhead Killer was trapped.

He envisioned the serial killer sneaking up on the undercover couple with hammer in hand, moving from tree to tree and hiding behind each one to regroup for his next move. The detective saw the Hammerhead Killer swinging his hammer a few feet away from his prey, but only grazing the male cop's face. Rossi remembered how his undercover team sprang to action and wrestled the killer to the ground, then slapped handcuffs on the man's wrists from behind his back.

But the manhunt's finale was most stunning to Detective Rossi, who visualized the police helicopters rapidly lowering, rotary wings circling, down on their man.

Does the Punishment Fit the Crimes?

Subsequent to getting caught, the Hammerhead Killer was arrested and indicted for murder. His trial for eight counts of murder in the first degree followed. The weapon justified the jury's guilty verdict that confined the man for life. Victims' hair and blood stains had soaked into the hammer's wooden handle and dried there, cementing the evidence for conviction.

Still, the defense had pleaded insanity, so the State sent the psychopath to Pilgrim State Hospital, a mental asylum on Crooked Road in Brentwood, Long Island. The hospital opened in 1931 and was named after Dr. Charles W. Pilgrim, formerly New York State Commissioner of Mental Health. The 800-acre state-run institution was once the largest mental health hospital in the nation.

In Building 23, before treatment reforms, patients were treated with controversial electric shock therapy and were lobotomized to provide relief from mental illness. Often, patients were left docile or, worse yet, lifeless. Eventually, the inhumane treatments gave way to greater use of psychiatric drugs to help cure the mentally ill at the renamed Pilgrim Psychiatric Center.

Over the years, acreage was sold to be repurposed, and some of its buildings became defunct and decayed, evoking a dark, brooding atmosphere. Drivers who take Exit 2 off the Sagtikos Parkway head toward the institution's remaining buildings and see the gloomy sight looming.

Pilgrim State's storied past still conjures spirited tales that attract seekers of the macabre to its grounds. One sordid story tells of patients buried in the back of the hospital. Like Potters Field, they are patients who are unknown, with no connection to family. It's been rumored that the Hammerhead Killer was buried there, but how he died is not public knowledge. The legend is that he was killed by a brain injury suffered from a frontal lobotomy gone wrong. If such malpractice did happen, many people might think that it was ironically befitting to the madman's crimes.

TEN

MOTIVES FOR MURDER AT THE VATICAN

The night after Heaton and Cole met Rossi, a meeting that may have triggered the detective's nightmares, both actors gathered with other cast members at the Little Theater to rehearse their lines about Juan Borgia's cold case murder at the Vatican.

Professor Lampton staged scene four with her show's narrator about investigating the killing of Pope Alexander's son, Juan.

Narrator (Gavin Cole), standing at the podium downstage left with minimal scenery: *Pope Alexander, still inconsolable about his favorite son's murder, was facing the horror of outliving his child, which is not the natural order of events. The Pope made inquiries as to who assassinated his son Juan, but strangely, the investigation stopped cold.* Addressing the audience: *You may ask why, but if you think twice about it, you may find your answer. Seemingly, the killer or person who ordered the assassination had been identified, but the Pope could not—or would not—take action because exposing the murderer would bring great harm to the papacy. The action backtracks to the rumors about who is responsible for the crime.*

"I see that you are following my direction about breath control," commented Professor Lampton. "You are projecting to the back row of your audience now. Just one new suggestion about saying the line 'You may ask why.' The line, of course, requests your audience to think, so you must make strong eye contact across various sections of your audience to engage everyone. Let's move on to scene five."

Juan's Mother (Celestine Houseman), in the Pope's chambers for official meetings, across from the Pope seated at his huge desk: *I've come to see you, Alexander, because I hear rumors about our son's murder spreading within the Vatican and through the streets of Rome.*

Pope Alexander (Wes Addison): *I wish that we could be meeting under better circumstances. We did share some very happy times. I still remember the day Juan was born. It was a joyous day! But now I am grieving like I never have after learning of his death. He was my favorite of our children. Maybe because he was most like me—ambitious but sensuous.*

Juan's Mother: *It's your favoritism that may be part of this problem. There's talk that Cesare is a suspect. He hated his brother, Juan, though you may not have seen it. Cesare has always resented having to follow you in the church. He preferred a military career, which Juan was offered. Even Queen Elizabeth of Spain believes Cesare is guilty, which means all the European courts will soon have their suspicions.*

Professor Lampton directed Addison to use his eyes more to express what he had been thinking, as Alexander's thoughts were not in the text. "Wes, the subtext of the dialogue between you and Celestine could be damning. In other words, if an investigation leads to naming a family member as Juan's killer, it would cause a big scandal. So, the investigation must stop, as the Pope should be careful about what he wishes to discover. Thus, I suggest you use your eyes more to express your thinking about a potential scandal. Your expressions will communicate more than the script's words."

"I understand," the actor acknowledged. "I've watched silent films and studied how actors used their eyes to communicate. Garbo was especially brilliant. She revealed all her emotions and thoughts in the script with her eyes."

"Excellent observation!" exclaimed Professor Lampton. "It seems we understand each other. Now, use that observation as we continue with the scene."

Pope Alexander: *Cesare never said a word to me about being dissatisfied. His anger will continue to eat at him. I will speak to him about letting his hatred go.*

Now, who else is being rumored as a suspect?

Juan's Mother: *Jofre. It is known that Juan slept with Jofre's wife. Many think that Jofre had his brother killed because of jealousy.*

Pope Alexander: *Did Juan leave your party that night to meet Jofre's wife? When we got the news of Juan's death, Lucrezia had said that he left the party to meet a woman.*

Juan's Mother: *I heard Juan setting out to meet Jofre's wife is the truth.*

Pope Alexander: *But do you know if Juan actually met her?*

Juan's Mother: *The rumor is that he spent time with her that night. An undisclosed source said that Juan was seen leaving her home just before his assassination. Jealousy always is a very strong emotion and motive for murder, especially when it comes to love and marriage.*

Pope Alexander: *But what about Milan's ruling family having a motive? Cesare and I were helping Lucrezia have her marriage to Giovanni annulled. Since Giovanni is connected to the Sforzas of Milan, the family most likely was feeling that our political alliance was waning.*

Juan's Mother: *It is true that the Sforzas were feeling cut off and wanting revenge. All suspects are viable, so I urge you to stop the investigation. You might learn something that will backfire on the Vatican.*

Professor Lampton stopped the scene. "You

both interpreted the lines truthfully. It's real. I feel the emotion and understand the dialogue's subtext, so let's end tonight's rehearsal on that positive note. I'd rather pace ourselves through the rehearsal process. I'll see you all tomorrow night to continue rehearsing at six-thirty sharp."

Afterward, the professor and her cast talked casually, mostly about going on the road with the show. Then, they all covered up for a cool fall night and paired off as they headed to the theater's door.

Cole and Heaton, again, left together. This time, Perrill watched the two actors, thinking, *I'd like to join them.* Perhaps she was thinking about Monty and Henry during the early '50s, when New York City was alive with excitement, when the threesome met for the first time and left Dotti Killian's house party together for breakfast. She had that feeling of déjà vu, then thought twice about leaving with the two actors. She felt unsure if something might be going on between them and didn't want to be a third wheel.

ELEVEN

SADDLING UP WITH DIANNA

Cole felt stressed balancing rehearsals, classes, and time spent with Heaton outside the Little Theater. To relax, he decided to take a walk. Initially, many thoughts raced through the young actor's mind, including where his relationship with Heaton was going. Walking alone in the quiet forest and smelling the pines helped clear his head, and he left the trees feeling at peace. Cole then went to the nearby horse stables, originally built by Dianna's family members when they acquired the estate decades before the college purchased it.

Suddenly, by coincidence, Cole stopped to see Dianna high on her horse that she still kept at the stables. The actress, who always turned heads, seemed breathtaking on her horse, perhaps because he was seeing her elevated. It was no wonder Dianna had been successful in Hollywood. Besides being a stunner, the woman had presence and really could act. Plus, Dianna came from a prominent family with connections.

As she trotted toward Cole, the young actor got a closer look at her. She was wearing a brown suede hat with a floppy brim, tilted slightly down on the right side of her forehead. Her dirty blond hair flowed from under the hat and blew in the autumn winds. She wore a green corduroy shirt with double-breasted pockets that accentuated her hazel eyes. Cole stared at Dianna's tight black jeans and brown leather boots that went up to her knees. What happened next surprised him.

"Come ride with me," Dianna said.

"I've only ridden a horse once in my life, so I'm out of practice," he replied, laughing.

"I mean, get up on my horse and ride behind me." Dianna's thin body allowed enough room for two in the saddle. "Just put your left foot in the stirrup and pull yourself up with your left hand by the saddle horn. Come on now! There's room for both of us."

Cole, though nervous about getting on a horse behind Dianna, followed his castmate's instructions. He boosted himself up and put his arms around her waist to hold on for the ride. He wondered where the conversation might lead.

"What have you learned about acting? Dianna asked, trotting along to ease Gavin into riding.

"I'm learning about using sense memory to feel emotions in the moment. I know Montgomery Clift was a Method actor trained in this technique by Marina."

"Well, I also have a lesson for you," said Dianna.

Where is she going with this? wondered Gavin.

"Working in a stage production takes commitment and focus. I see you're hanging around Henry, who could be distracting. Running lines together outside rehearsal is good reinforcement, but I know Henry has more on his mind. I know him well."

Gavin understood more than Dianna was saying.

"Anyway, hold on to me tighter. I'm going to run him a little." Dianna galloped her horse across a field behind the stables.

Gripping her, Gavin thought this would be a perfect time to get Dianna's perspective about Heaton. "How did Marina feel about Henry and Monty seeing each other? I know they were together during most of Monty's career. Henry told me he always loved him."

Dianna kept riding without breaking stride. "Marina was jealous of Henry. She wanted Monty for herself, so she could coach him without Henry interfering. I think she loved him too, though it wasn't sexual for more than a couple of decades. They had a brief affair when they first met on Broadway in 1942, but that changed when she started coaching him."

"Did you also love Monty?" asked Gavin. "Henry explained how the three of you met at Dotti Killian's house party in the early 1950s."

Slowing her horse to a halt, Dianna turned to Gavin. "Yes, I did love him. Monty was so good looking before his car accident and very slight and slim. Both men and women loved him. He was an exciting, magnetic actor who made everything come alive."

"So, what happened to your relationship?"

Dianna didn't answer until she gathered her thoughts. "Monty had two sides. He was an incredible human being but had a dark side. For me, he became more and more difficult to be with on a regular basis, especially after his car crash. He was unhappy with his face after the surgery, which was needed due to the accident. His face was partially paralyzed, and his mouth could not move easily. He used his eyes more than ever to act, and they held a haunted look. You could see how Monty's face changed in *The Young Lions*, the first movie he made after *Raintree County*, which was being filmed during the time of his accident."

Cole noted that he knew of Monty's car accident, but he was not aware of the physical and psychological impact of the surgery. "Go on—tell me more," he urged.

"To complete shooting *Raintree County*, they shot around his face. Monty hated looking at himself and wouldn't even have mirrors at home. Then his drinking became dangerous. That's when we drifted apart, though Henry and Marina, to their credit, stuck with him until he died."

Dianna looked to the sky and saw storm clouds rolling over the campus. "We better head back before it starts pouring," she said. As the first raindrops hit her hat's brim, she signaled the horse to trot.

After they dismounted, Cole walked along as

Dianna led her horse to the stables, realizing a newfound respect for Henry and Marina for staying with Monty to the end. Marina, of course, was getting a cut of Monty's movie salary for coaching him, but Henry had stayed with him purely for love.

Joe Buck and Ratso

By happenstance, *Midnight Cowboy*, which Heaton had encouraged Cole to see, was being shown that day at the campus's new student auditorium. When the rain got heavier, Gavin and Dianna parted, and the young actor ran to see the late afternoon matinee. Feeling especially emotional about the ending, he watched Dustin Hoffman's character, Ratso, die of tuberculosis on a Miami-bound bus to warmer weather. Cole welled up watching Jon Voight's Joe Buck put his arm around his dead friend. For Cole, the scene captured Joe's love and compassion, mirroring Heaton's last days with Clift before he died. Cole finally understood the reason Heaton identified so much with the classic film.

TWELVE

MAN GONE MISSING

That rainy night after the movie, Cole ran back to his dormitory to change into dry clothes, causing him to be fifteen minutes late for a 6:30 rehearsal. He joined the other cast members, who were all there except for Heaton. Professor Lampton, thinking he might be stuck in traffic, decided to wait until 7:00 before starting. Still, Henry didn't appear.

Professor Lampton was concerned. "Has anyone seen Henry or heard from him since our last rehearsal?"

After some silence, while the cast looked at each other for answers, Cole spoke up. "I was with him the day before yesterday at the police station in Old Westbury. We went to see Detective Rossi, who's investigating Trish O'Leary's murder that took place on campus last June. Henry had confided with me about being on campus the day Trish was killed and seeing a woman who looked suspicious, so I suggested Henry talk to the detective about what he witnessed. It's a long story, but I haven't seen him since then."

Professor Lampton went to the theater's office to call Henry at home. *Maybe he forgot about the rehearsal and was sleeping*, she thought, as the phone kept ringing. But Henry didn't answer, and the director hung up, thinking, *possibly he's still stuck in traffic*. When she returned to the cast and crew, they were speculating about a car accident on a slick road in the rain.

An accident would be ironic, considering Monty's collision, thought Gavin.

After rehearsing without Henry, Professor Lampton felt it was time to call the Old Westbury police station about Heaton's whereabouts, since the actor recently met with Detective Rossi there. Lampton returned to the theater's office to call, first sitting, then nervously standing, while the phone rang. In an emergency such as this, she was not the collected professor who appeared in class.

"Old Westbury police station," answered the desk sergeant. "How can I help you?"

"This is Professor Lampton at Old Westbury College." The professor paused to be clear about her reply. "I would like to report a missing person, a cast member of a show I'm directing at the college. He was supposed to be at the campus's theater for our six-thirty rehearsal this evening."

"What's his name?" asked the desk sergeant.

"Henry Heaton. You may have heard of him. He's

a known actor around Glen Cove, where he lives, and surrounding towns. And, coincidentally, he met the day before yesterday with your Detective Rossi."

"Yes, I've heard of him. I remember him being at the station, but there's not much we can do right now. Protocol is that we wait twenty-four hours before filing a missing person report for someone over eighteen. Most missing people show up before then. We get too many calls to respond to each one immediately."

His explanation frustrated Professor Lampton, and she let out a heavy sigh.

"For a child twelve and under, we'll investigate at once. If the reported missing person is a teenager, we'll wait a little longer, knowing that sometimes teens are beginning to rebel at home and will act irresponsibly. Let's see where we stand in the next twenty-four hours. If you hear from Mr. Heaton during that time, let us know. And, of course, if you don't connect with him in that time frame, call the station. Thank you for being patient, professor. Do you have any other questions?"

"No," Professor Lampton conceded. "I suppose my hands are tied for now. Thank you for your time." The professor hung up the phone, feeling disillusioned about the police always ready to help, yet intellectually she understood the logic of the protocol.

Rather than wait for Heaton to make contact, Professor Lampton continued calling throughout most of the night and next day, but there was no connection with the missing actor. Knowing Henry's penchant for men, Professor Lampton wondered if he met a new man and disappeared, neglecting rehearsals. Twenty-four hours passed without word from him, and the continuing rain added to her dreary mood. Lampton called the Old Westbury station house again to report that nobody had heard from Henry and he could not be reached by phone. A missing person report was filed with all the necessary details that included last seen whereabouts, places that Henry typically frequented, and any person who recently had been in contact with him, such as Cole and Detective Rossi.

After getting Heaton's address from the professor, two patrol cars were dispatched to his Glen Cove home to investigate. As the officers circled the home looking for anything unusual, they noticed the side door was slightly open. An officer knocked on it several times without an answer, then the officers entered the home, believing that an open door and getting no response after knocking was a bad sign.

Finding Monty

The officers were astonished to see the many framed photos around the cottage. "Wow, this is kind of odd!" said one officer, pointing to the pictures. "That's Montgomery Clift, the famous movie actor! Wonder what was going on here? He's been dead for a number of years." But nobody had answers. They just stared at the photos, perplexed about what looked like an obsession.

"I found shoe prints in blood leading from a room," shouted another officer. The prints were eerily similar to the shoe prints outside Trish's dormitory room. When the officers entered the bedroom, they found Henry sprawled on the bed with his shirt unbuttoned, exposing wounds and blood that had coagulated on his chest. Appearing to have been dressing for the previous night's rehearsal, the actor's clothes were bloodied from stabbings, and his head was bludgeoned. A picture of Monty in a metal frame lay on the floor next to the bed. The frame and glass encasing the picture were full of blood, too. Seemingly, the corner of the metal frame had been weaponized to pound Henry's head.

Henry had left himself vulnerable. The officers saw the bedroom window had been left open, allowing the rain to come inside the room. This was the same window with broken locks that Henry hadn't had time to fix. At first glance, officers at the scene believed the window was the pathway to murder.

"Call dispatch—get homicide here," said the sergeant to another officer, "and tell them to send a team from Glen Cove's station house, too." Since Heaton was killed there, the town's police investigative team would have to get involved.

The officer returned to his patrol car to get on the radio. "We've got a Code 55-A. Send our homicide team to the home on the corner of Landing Road and Germaine Street in Glen Cove. And contact Glen Cove's station house to send a team here. We have a male victim, approximately early- to mid-forties, dead in the home. He's been knifed, and his head has been bludgeoned. We believe he's Henry Heaton, the home's resident, who was reported missing earlier. We understand he was a community theater actor who performed in Glen Cove and its nearby towns."

Just as Heaton was growing excited about a new production, he would have to be replaced in Professor Lampton's show.

THIRTEEN

LIGHTNING STRIKES TWICE FOR DETECTIVE ROSSI

The side door to Heaton's home remained open. Nothing should be changed in a crime scene investigation so potential physical evidence is not tainted or destroyed. Though the murder occurred in Glen Cove, the town's police investigation team was willing to be a cooperating partner in the case. Detective Rossi was assigned, once again, as the lead detective on this new murder case. The detective drew the assignment because he was one of the few people known to have last spoken with Heaton and was familiar with the actor's suspicious revelation at the dollhouse.

All the while, a neighbor who lived across the street from Heaton was observing the commotion. Detective Rossi, with his keen eye for details, saw a pair of spectacles peering through the blinds. Before interviewing the neighbor, however, Rossi first wanted to get a sense of what took place inside Henry's home.

Detective Rossi entered the kitchen through the open side door. He was followed by a few other detectives and an entourage from his forensics team, equipped with their investigative tools. Accompanied by detectives from both station houses and his technical team, Rossi questioned the sergeant, one of the first officers at the crime scene.

"What's your overall sense of what happened here?" he asked.

The sergeant led Rossi and everyone under his leadership to the bloody footprints. "The prints are facing outward from the bedroom. That's the room where we discovered the victim dead on his bed. He's been stabbed multiple times all over his body, and his head has been bludgeoned. It seems that's where he was killed."

Detective Rossi agreed, seeing the prints were pointing toe-cap-to-heel toward them from the bedroom.

Forensics began taping around the footprints with bright yellow, non-adhesive abatement tape to preserve the evidence for dusting. Meanwhile, Detective Rossi, another detective from Glen Cove's station, and other forensics team members entered the bedroom. Seeing Heaton's body on the bed, Detective Rossi quietly observed the scene without saying anything until he collected himself.

"I just spoke to Heaton two days ago about the O'Leary murder and what he witnessed the day she was killed. Now, he's also stabbed multiple times. It's uncanny!"

Rossi noted specific similarities between the murders. The angle of the knife breaking Heaton's skin suggested his killer was left-handed, just like Trish's attacker.

Working to prevent contaminating evidence, the technical team used the same yellow tape to create a barrier around Henry's body.

"Okay, let's get photos of the victim," directed Detective Rossi.

A crime scene photographer began taking many angled photos of the victim. Accurate pictures are critical to a criminal investigation because detectives, like Rossi, and jurors can study the pictures to understand what happened, even months or years after a crime. Pictures of the stab wounds would greatly help a prosecutor prove in court the killer is left-handed.

After photos were taken, Detective Rossi went to the open window, where the rain splashed his face. "The window's glass pane isn't broken, so it seems it was unlocked," he noted to another detective in the room. "We'll have forensics investigate it." Then, Rossi stuck his head out the window to see a garden, muddy from the rain. Pulling his head back inside, he turned to examine the bedroom carpet. "There's mud on the carpet," continued Rossi. "It's clear this killer entered through the window and brought mud inside," he said as he pointed to the mud stains.

"What's the significance?" asked the sergeant, a step or two behind Rossi.

"We can suspect this attacker came in through that window but exited out the side door, since it was left open," Rossi explained. "And that's the key!"

"How so?" the sergeant persisted.

"There's a neighbor watching from the house directly opposite the side door to Heaton's home," replied Rossi. "I saw someone peeping from a window. We must find out what the neighbor might have witnessed—if this neighbor did see anyone, it would have been a full-frontal view, and that's vitally significant!"

Shifting attention to the floor near the bedside, everyone focused on the picture of Monty in the blood-soaked frame. Possibly, it had been the weapon that caused Heaton's final death blow, but only forensics could determine whether the frame's point contributed to ending Henry's life. The picture frame also had been encircled with yellow tape and was being dusted for fingerprints.

"What do you think is going on with all these photos of Montgomery Clift?" the sergeant asked Rossi.

"Some of these pictures are pretty intimate, and I heard Clift was bi-sexual."

There was momentary silence after Rossi's statement. Some officers thought, *do we have a gay murder?* Detective Rossi wondered, *perhaps a jealous lover saw Heaton running around with that college boy.*

"Let's visit that peeper across the street now," said

Detective Rossi, cynically.

Accompanied by a few other detectives, he knocked on the neighbor's door. Sticking his head through the doorway, the peeper's horn-rimmed eyeglasses stood out above an impish grin.

"I'm Detective Rossi, here with my team of detectives. Can we step inside to talk?" Face-to-face, Rossi realized the neighbor was a man, despite his slight frame.

"What's this about?" the neighbor inquired timidly, his voice quavering.

"It's about your neighbor, Henry Heaton, being murdered in his home."

The neighbor didn't respond at first, as he was digesting Rossi's blunt delivery of the news. Nevertheless, the man didn't act shocked because he knew of Henry's lifestyle. After inviting the detectives inside his home, he was ready to answer any questions that might help the investigation.

"I saw you looking through your blinds earlier, when I arrived with my team," said Rossi.

"Oh, well, I was checking the weather," replied the neighbor offhandedly. "I heard hard rain on my skylight."

The detective eyed the peeper skeptically. He saw a fiftyish runt of a man, with limp, graying brown hair that was parted on the side. Standing about five feet, six inches and hunched over, his ungroomed mustache and high-pitched voice irritated Rossi. Ironically, he reminded the detective of character actor Wally Cox, who starred in *Mister Peepers*, the 1950s television show.

"Were you looking out that same window yesterday, around late afternoon or early evening, and did you notice anything unusual?" asked Detective Rossi.

The peeper stopped to think about his answer, so not to appear like a spying neighbor, though he liked to watch. He lived alone, so watching filled his time. "I looked out my window after hearing the weather report and thunder. I saw storm clouds. Guess it seemed unusual that I noticed a woman leaving Henry's home. Usually, I saw men coming out the side door. You see, I knew about Henry. I've been living here a long time, going back to the mid-fifties. I remember seeing that actor—Montgomery Clift—going in and out of Henry's home for years. I couldn't miss seeing him. I had seen his movies throughout the fifties and early sixties."

"Can you describe this woman?" Rossi asked, digging for more.

"She was tall. But I can't identify much about her because it was dark and raining, and she was wearing a raincoat with a hood."

The detective seemed puzzled. "If you couldn't see too much, how do you know you saw a woman?"

"I just felt it; something about the way she moved. So, do you think this woman killed Henry?"

"I don't know. That's the reason we're investi-gating. But thank you for your assistance. Here's my card. Call me if you think of anything else that might help us."

The neighbor lingered at his doorway as he watched Detective Rossi lead his team of detectives back to Heaton's home. There, Rossi shared a clever investigative tool with his detectives. "Usually, a killer either takes something from a crime scene or leaves something behind. Whatever that may be, it could be the lynchpin to solving this murder and getting an arrest and a conviction."

So, a thorough search was made throughout Henry's home to find something. Overlooked earlier was a half pack of Marlboro Gold cigarettes on the kitchen floor near the side door. Rossi discovered the pack, and he knew that it most likely belonged to the purported killer because there were no ashtrays seen around Heaton's home. Thus, any person of interest found smoking Marlboro Gold could become a primary suspect.

Rossi and his squad moved back to Heaton's bedroom. After rummaging through Heaton's walk-in closet, one detective found a manuscript written by the actor. After giving the manuscript to his boss, Detective Rossi flipped through the pages and saw it was a draft for a tell-all book. There was juicy content, including chapters about Monty, Marina, and Dianna.

The detective knew about Henry's role in Professor Lampton's play since the actor had met with him to discuss the O'Leary case. Interviewing cast members was in order to expose persons of interest or, even better, a suspect in the murder investigation. They had motives and means to explore.

FOURTEEN

THE SHOW MUST GO ON

Professor Lampton quickly replaced Heaton in the cast. Some cast members thought the swift replacement seemed callous to Henry's memory, but the show had been booked in three cities and had to go on tour as planned to meet the scheduled dates. Like Heaton, the newly hired actor had performed in community theater, where the director first saw him and established a professional relationship. Known by his stage name, Bob Boswell, he looked very different from Henry. He was a big man and cherubic-looking, with a clean-shaven face of baby-smooth skin.

When he was introduced to the cast and crew by Professor Lampton at the next rehearsal, Cole recognized him as the man who was at the door during his lunch at Heaton's place and thought, *this is a strange twist.*

With the approaching show, Boswell had to be a quick study of the script and his lines. Finally, after a period of adjustment for the cast and crew and rehearsing several more times, the director was ready to open the show in Pittsburgh.

Cast and crew, Professor Lampton, and Marina Rostova, who was continuing to coach Cole, were all excited about going on the road. Of course, both professors would have their classes covered. They met at New York City's underground Penn Station near the concourse level's information desk. After Professor Lampton arranged everyone's transportation at the Amtrak ticket window, the theater group walked to their track and boarded the train to Pittsburgh. Once seated, small groups talked about the New York theater, Hollywood, the art of acting, and their private lives. Nobody mentioned Henry's murder, as the subject still was fresh and uncomfortable to discuss, but everyone had to be thinking of him.

Late in the afternoon, the train pulled into Pittsburgh's Union Station. Outside, taxis formed a line ready to take passengers throughout the city. Members of the production split up and took cabs to the historic William Penn Hotel, where they would stay overnight and get ready for the next day's opening matinee.

Cole, new to the road and impressionable, was amazed at the grandeur of their hotel, once the world's second largest structure. He was impressed by the hotel's famous facade, modeled after the Beaux-Arts. The architecture showcased classic Greek and Roman decorative features like columns, pediments, and balustrades to create something imposing.

Checking in to their rooms in assigned pairs, Cole learned he would be sharing a room, reluctantly, with Boswell. After everyone took their luggage up to their rooms, they met at the hotel's main restaurant for dinner, pre-celebrating the show's opening on Professor Lampton's expense account. Orders were taken, then various aromas filled the room as the wait staff carried out entrées of steak, chicken, and fish. Red and white wine were served, relaxing everyone and stimulating talk across adjoining tables.

Still, nobody brought up Henry's murder. Instead, they spoke about the Watergate hearings, which had taken place that summer. "How do you think it will end for Nixon?" asked Professor Rostova, who, coming from Russia, was especially interested in American politics.

"The hearings could lead to his impeachment, or he may resign in disgrace before that process starts," replied Boswell, who, being new to the cast, wanted to make his voice heard.

"Well, I'm glad this administration is under fire for breaking in to the Democratic National Committee office," added Professor Lampton, a known liberal on campus.

"But know this: both parties have looked for dirt on the opposing party," pointed out Boswell. "The Nixon administration just got caught. And that's the difference."

After dinner, everyone involved in the show went in different directions. Older members of the production went to their rooms to rest for the next day's opening, while others left the hotel for a change of scenery.

Dianna, who had enjoyed some intimacy riding with Cole, invited the young actor for a nightcap. Not wanting to wander, they went to the hotel bar, where they could talk privately, away from the group. Dianna ordered an Absolute vodka martini with two olives. She especially liked the martini-soaked olives. Gavin got a Seven and Seven on ice, which he had first enjoyed at high school parties. Sipping their drinks, they began discussing the excitement and nervousness of the show's opening, especially the rush felt from applause and jitters that cause nausea for some actors.

Then the conversation transitioned, and Dianna urged Gavin to stay focused. "Don't get distracted by Bob Boswell," she warned. "Don't let him lure you."

Gavin played it coy. "What do you mean?"

"He's a predator. I heard about him. Do you understand me?"

Gavin shifted in his chair as he reacted to Dianna's bluntness, then nodded to show that her message resonated with him.

Dianna changed the subject again. "I've been curious about your timing during the afternoon of Henry's murder," she said.

"What timing are you talking about?"

"You were fifteen minutes late for rehearsal the

day Henry was killed. What happened?"

The young actor had no idea where she was going with her comment but was instantly defensive. "What are you insinuating?"

"Were you with Henry at his home the afternoon he was murdered?"

"Absolutely not!" he replied, emphatically. "After riding with you, I went to see the *Midnight Cowboy* matinee at the new student auditorium. But I got caught in the rain coming out from the show, so I ran back to my dorm room to put on dry clothes. That's the reason I was late." Gavin's resolute tone ended the conversation at the bar.

Finishing their drinks, the actors walked together to the hotel elevator. At their floor, they parted ways, but Gavin was apprehensive when he reached his room. Getting the door key out of his pocket, he didn't know what to expect from his roommate.

Before he opened the door, he stopped. He was ambivalent about reacting to the so-called aggressor in his room. *Will I react diplomatically if Boswell puts a move on me?* he questioned himself. To avoid confrontation, Gavin went back to the hotel bar, where he ordered another Seven and Seven to numb himself. After having his drink, Gavin moved to the hotel's common area where guests could relax. There, he dozed in a leather chair until morning, but didn't sleep very well with Boswell on his mind.

When Gavin woke the next morning, he knew

confronting Bob was necessary to move on with the show. Without overthinking it, he went to his room, but Boswell was not there. Instead, he found a note saying his roommate had gone to breakfast but would be coming back shortly.

Gavin, anticipating coming face-to-face with Boswell at any moment, took a hot shower, dressed, and ordered room service. Sipping on his black coffee, the young actor heard the key turning in the door, and he felt stressed. Boswell walked inside, and the two actors' eyes locked.

"Where were you last night?" asked Bob.

"I had a drink at the bar and sat down in the hotel's common area, where I fell asleep."

Boswell, to Gavin's surprise, put the young actor at ease. "Would you like to run lines before getting into makeup and costume for the opening?" he asked.

The idea of running lines, as Gavin had with Henry, broke the young actor's tension. His muscles relaxed, and he smiled. "Sure, that will help quiet my nerves."

After running through their lines in their hotel room, they met everyone from the troupe in the hotel lobby. Professor Lampton had hired a private bus to transport everyone to the theater, which was on a college campus; she had arranged the stage space through her academic connections.

While getting into makeup and costume, Cole started feeling queasy. It appeared to be stage fright, made worse by his previous night's drinking and anxiety over Boswell. In the bathroom of the green room, Cole washed his face, combed his hair, and gargled with mouthwash that had been left there. He was ready to perform, though still feeling the usual nerves of an opening.

Nevertheless, Cole's performance thrilled him. Being in front of an audience and hearing the applause, no longer just running lines and rehearsing, reinforced his hunger for acting. Cole knew for sure that he had found his career calling.

After the elation at the theater, everyone from the production went back to their hotel rooms to get ready for dinner, followed by a short evening, as they had to take an early morning train to Worcester, Massachusetts, where they would be performing next.

Once in their room, Boswell began questioning Cole. "So, do you have a girlfriend on campus?"

"Well, no. I had liked a girl who lived in my dormitory, but she was stabbed in her room last June. I'm sure you know about Trish O'Leary's murder. Most everybody heard the story."

"Yes, the story was all over the news. I especially followed the *Times-Journal* reporting. The description of her killing was difficult to read. I can tell that her murder continues to deeply affect you. I see it on your face." Cole turned away, ending the conversation.

He looked around their hotel room in dismay. The room only had a queen-size bed, and the roll-away Cole had requested at the front desk never came. The actors had to share a bed.

Sometime during the middle of the night, Cole felt Boswell move closer and rub against him. "Stay away from me!" Cole yelled, pushing Boswell off the bed.

Hitting the floor with a thud, the heavyset actor got the message and looked up at Gavin apologetically. "Okay, it's over. I just thought...you know, the way you ran around with Henry."

"You know nothing about our relationship," Cole snapped. "How can you insinuate anything about us?" His strong words and tone stunned the shot-down actor, who remained flat on his back.

Cole rose from the bed. "I'm going to the bathroom," he said. His mouth was dry from the sour taste caused by Boswell. After brushing his teeth, Gavin walked back to his side of the bed. There, he paused, unsure about Boswell's behavior. *I have an early morning train ride and tomorrow's performance*, he thought. *I need a good night's sleep.* Cole got into bed, trusting his roommate would stay on his side. And he did.

Despite the actors' conflict, they continued to perform well together on the road in Worcester and Wooster. Gavin learned that a true professional must overcome personal distraction on stage, and his acting improved with each performance.

After the show's close at Wooster, the tight bond that developed among the cast and crew on the road naturally dissipated as everyone went back to their separate lives.

FIFTEEN

THE PRIMARY PERSON OF INTEREST

Anxious to interview selected production members who were becoming persons of interest in Heaton's murder, Detective Rossi summoned Dianna Perrill first. She was contacted to arrange a meeting with Rossi at Old Westbury's station house as soon as possible. Not wanting to have the ordeal hanging over her head, the actress reacted quickly to meet with the top detective.

Perrill entered Detective Rossi's office oozing self-confidence. It was the same confidence the actress displayed on stage and film. Anyone could tell that her body language, especially the way she walked, showed strength and style, qualities inherent to most of the rich and famous. She was not lawyered up, as that would have signaled a defensive posture and contradicted her self-confidence.

Still, Perrill had a motive and the means. She had

learned about Heaton's tell-all book during a confrontation with the actor just prior to his murder, and being rich, she could have easily hired someone to do her dirty work.

"Have a seat and relax," said Detective Rossi.

Though she may not have felt relaxed under the circumstances, Perrill knew how to act calm. That was part of her theater training.

"I heard the show went well on the road," remarked Rossi, looking to break the ice.

Perrill shrugged. "Let's cut the small talk, detective. What do you want to know?"

"Okay, let's do it," Rossi replied, about to start his cat-and-mouse game. "What do you know about Heaton's book manuscript?"

Perrill looked surprised that Rossi knew about it. "How did you find out about his manuscript?" she asked. The Hollywood star's tone showed that her calm attitude had been penetrated.

"I thought I was asking the questions," Rossi countered in his typical snarky way, "but if you must know, we discovered Heaton's manuscript while investigating the crime scene the day after his murder. Now, please address my question."

"Okay," conceded Perrill. "I first learned of Henry's manuscript when he approached me about it. He told me he had been writing a memoir about his love affair with Montgomery Clift, the actor, and that he needed money, as his acting career was declining.

Monty was a big movie star for most of his career, and the story about Henry's long-standing, secret affair with him would have certainly attracted a publisher and readers."

Detective Rossi had read the manuscript, so he understood Dianna's point about it easily attracting an audience. After seeing how the manuscript shed a controversial spotlight on Perrill, Rossi believed he uncovered circumstantial evidence linking the actress to Heaton's murder.

"Part of the manuscript includes your own affair with Clift," said the detective, looking into Perrill's eyes. "It's clear from the manuscript that Clift was bi-sexual, and the real damning part points to you and Clift and Henry together sexually, with the three of you at a naked pool party on your family's estate. It's circumstantial evidence, of course, but it gives you a motive. I could see how you would be desperate to stop publication of that book."

Although Hollywood had aways been sexually progressive behind the scenes, taboos that were broken and made public wrecked careers. Perrill feared that, so she attempted to stop its publication. "Henry wanted two million dollars from me in exchange for not publishing the manuscript. At first, I tried to equalize his scheme, making it clear the book would harm him, too. Homosexuals are not widely accepted publicly, as you know. One day that might change, but not in 1973."

"So, did Henry back off on publishing?" asked

Detective Rossi.

"No. The stubborn son-of-a-bitch told me, 'I don't care about exposing myself. I know I'm selling out, but I must use what I've got to survive, and this is my ticket.'"

"So, you had no way out," observed Detective Rossi.

Perrill threw her hands in the air. "I had no choice but promise to pay him."

Rossi checked his notes to be sure he was on point. "How did you know Henry would not come back asking for more money? That's a blackmailer's game."

"I threatened to have him killed if he returned wanting more money," Dianna confessed. "It was the only card left to play, in my mind, but I never would have followed through with murder. I did not kill Henry! I have no clue who did, but whoever killed him did me a great favor. So, if you are not going to arrest me, I guess I'm free to go."

No arrest was made, and Perrill confidently rose from her chair and walked out of Detective Rossi's office like she was performing for the camera. She never even looked back. She's a real cool one, Rossi thought.

SIXTEEN

WHAT MIGHT
MARINA KNOW?

Marina Rostova had been jealous of Henry throughout his relationship with Monty; it was only natural. She believed Henry distracted her from molding Monty's acting career, and the Russian acting coach loved Monty in her way. Because she was tied to both men, Detective Rossi believed Rostova might know something about Heaton's murder.

Shortly after grilling Dianna Perrill, the detective requested that Rostova come to Old Westbury's station house to be interviewed. She arrived by taxi and approached the desk sergeant to inquire about her appointment. Moments later, the detective got up from his desk to greet Rostova, extending his hand and showing reverence for the charismatic Russian.

"Please have a seat, Miss Rostova. Can I get you coffee or tea, or maybe something cold?"

Instinctively, Rostova believed accepting any offer might appear too friendly, making her feel obligated to explain more than she needed. "No, thank you," she said demurely in her Russian accent. "I know I'm here to discuss Henry's murder. What can I do for you, detective?"

Before Rossi replied, he looked closer at Marina. *She must have been quite attractive as a young woman*, he thought. *I can tell by the angles of her face, and those blue eyes are magnetic. She still looks good, even with her white hair.* The detective was attracted to Rostova's charisma despite her age, but he knew it was police business first. "Tell me about your relationship with Montgomery Clift."

Rostova didn't quite know how to begin, as their liaison was complicated. "When we first met on the New York stage in 1942, we had instant chemistry. I fell in love with Monty. He was striking and talented."

Rossi sensed their relationship evolved. "From what I understand, there were complications with Clift," commented the detective.

"It changed when I committed to coaching his acting, shortly after we met. It was like being married, but not romantically speaking. It was more like an artistic marriage. I coached him on every film and stayed with him on set, despite being disliked by some temperamental directors. I experienced all of Monty's good and bad times, including his car accident that affected him severely, personally and professionally."

"I heard about that accident," acknowledged Rossi. "I saw some of Clift's films in the early '60s, such as *The Misfits* and *Judgement at Nuremberg*, and his facial features didn't look as refined as in his earlier films. I'm sure he had great difficulty recovering." Rossi looked at Rostova for a reaction and saw her blue eyes turn watery.

"He never fully recovered," replied Marina. "Eventually drugs and alcohol killed him. I lost a big part of myself when he died, as I was wrapped up in his life. I've continued coaching other well-known actors, but it hasn't been the same."

Rossi looked down, feeling uncomfortable about his next question. "I'm about to ask a question that you might feel is personal and insensitive." He raised his head and looked directly at Marina. "But I must ask, as it's critical to the investigation."

Rostova gave no response.

"How did you feel about Heaton, knowing of his love for Montgomery?"

Rostova looked perturbed, though she expected the question. "How would you know about their relationship? It wasn't made public."

"I'm a detective," quipped Rossi. "It's my job to know. Seriously, we found Heaton's unpublished manuscript at his home, the day after he was murdered there. It was written as a memoir, mostly about his long relationship with Montgomery. We classified it as circumstantial evidence."

"I had no idea about the manuscript," said Rostova. "We had lunch last June, in fact on the same day that young girl was killed on campus, but Henry never mentioned his manuscript."

"I'm aware you met that day."

"During lunch, we talked about our mutual memories of Monty, naturally. I suppose he didn't discuss his manuscript to avoid my comments about its content."

"Were you really struggling with the relationship between Montgomery and Henry, as described in the manuscript?"

Rostova, understanding the interview was getting more personal, wanted to be truthful. The acting coach knew if she wasn't honest, it would seem that she was covering up something—and that would cast suspicion on her. "It's true Monty's long affair with Henry, though on and off, irritated me. I believed it was destructive for Monty, being mostly a sexual addiction. I saw he felt conflicted, which distracted him from our work. Despite their affection for each other, they argued over relationships outside their own. Henry especially was troubled over Monty's love for Liz Taylor. And Monty hated Henry's flings with younger men."

Rostova's mention of "younger men" reinforced what Detective Rossi had been thinking. *Might Cole have played a role, either directly or indirectly, in Heaton's murder?* "Did Heaton ever say anything about Gavin Cole to you?"

The charismatic coach wanted to be honest but careful with her words. "Henry said he had been running lines with Gavin to prepare for the show that just closed. You know about the show, of course? Henry was replaced in the cast with Bob Boswell, whom Henry had known from his group of homosexual friends and acquaintances. Do you think there's any connection among Henry, Boswell, and young Cole?"

Detective Rossi raised his eyebrow. At the same time, he doodled a triangle on his notepad, noting the three actors at the triangle's points. "We'll have to investigate a possible link." He began tapping his pen on the doodle. Rossi knew he soon would be bringing Cole in for questioning. "I believe that will be all for today," concluded the detective. "I'd be happy to drive you back to the college or your residence."

This time, the Russian professor accepted his offer, as she had grown more comfortable with him. "I'd like that. You can drive me back to campus. I have afternoon classes."

SEVENTEEN

MAN IN THE MIDDLE

Gavin Cole stood between two actors who had been involved in the show—and both men left their mark on him. But while the young actor may have encouraged his relationship with Henry Heaton, his connection to Bob Boswell was discouraged. Together, the three men provoked suspicion that Heaton's murder might be traced back to their relationships.

This triangle had been on Detective Rossi's mind, so he wanted to investigate further by questioning Cole. To prepare, he connected the dots in his notes and circled common denominators.

Cole returned to Old Westbury's station house to share his truth with Detective Rossi. After greeting the desk sergeant, the young actor was sent to Rossi's office. He knocked on the door, and the detective invited Cole to sit. Again, Cole found himself staring at the faces of wanted criminals posted on the wall behind the desk.

The meeting was not adversarial, as the two men

had been acquainted with each other. "I know you've been studying acting with Marina Rostova, who helped prepare you for the show that just ended," said Rossi. "It's impressive, considering she coached Montgomery Clift who became a big star!"

Cole already had realized his special fate. "I suppose I'm in good company."

"You seem to be in the middle of everything," joked the detective. "So, because of your relationship to Heaton and others in the show's cast, you may know something critical to solving Heaton's murder; you just may not realize it yet. My job is to draw that out of you."

I wonder what that might be? thought Gavin. "I'd like to cooperate so I can see closure in Henry's murder."

"First, can you describe your relationship with Heaton?" asked Rossi.

"We just were good friends," Cole replied abruptly.

"Are you sure you're not leaving anything out? I know about Heaton's sexual preference and his long affair with Montgomery Clift."

Cole clearly knew what Rossi was trying to pry from him. "Okay, I felt Henry was attracted to me. I could tell by his body language and could read between the lines of our conversations, but he never outwardly expressed his attraction. There just were veiled indications."

"Did you ever tell Heaton to back off from you?" the detective asked, still trying to get Cole to open up.

"No! It never came to that." Cole paused in thought. "However, the situation might have eventually called for me to be more assertive, if Henry hadn't been killed first."

"Can you tell me about Bob Boswell? I heard from my sources that you shared a hotel room with him while performing on the road. That's pretty close contact."

Rossi struck a nerve, so the young actor minimized his reply. "Nothing happened."

"I sense Boswell wanted more than just to be roommates," deduced Detective Rossi. "I'll leave that for you to ponder," said Cole. But Rossi had his mind on a bigger picture. "Okay, let's turn to Heaton and Boswell. I heard rumors they were seeing each other beyond being friends. Can you confirm the rumor?"

"I cannot confirm any rumor, but I was at Henry's place running lines with him for the show when Boswell knocked on the door. Henry went to the door and opened it, but he didn't invite Boswell in his home. I couldn't understand what they were saying, as their discussion was hushed, but it was clear the conversation got heated. Then I saw Henry nudge Boswell away— not pushing him hard, though, just enough to send a message that the big guy had stopped by at the wrong time and place."

Cole's testimony triggered a strong motive that suggested Boswell may have been a spurned lover. "Do you believe Boswell may have been jealous of you?" asked Rossi. "After all, you were stealing his time with

Heaton. Did you hear anything more, from Heaton or Boswell, about their confrontation at the door?"

Cole was unable to encourage further speculation. "Neither of them had spoken about the incident."

Detective Rossi seemed to progress in investigating persons of interest involving Heaton's murder. Except for circumstantial evidence, however, he still did not have solid proof to single out a primary suspect. The case remained cold, just like Trish O'Leary's case, and the detective continued having restless sleep.

EIGHTEEN

THE PHILOSOPHY PROFESSOR'S ALIBI

Detective Rossi lay on his back in bed, staring at the ceiling. Feeling restless, he turned on his left side for a short time and then on his right side. And then he rolled onto his back again. Still Rossi could not sleep, so he got up to get his favorite cognac at the liquor cabinet. The empty bottle of Courvoisier reminded him that he was coming up empty on both murder cases. Instead of cognac, Rossi poured a shot of Scotch to relax. After gulping it down, he went back to bed.

The detective felt physically less edgy, but his mind still raced. An image of Trish O'Leary curled up on her dorm room floor, motionless and bloodied, came to mind. Her image provoked thoughts of Gibby, the elusive guitarist who was nowhere to be found. Surely Gibby, who knew Trish from their nights working at the Rathskeller, exhibited strange behavior. It seemed the guitarist had no clear motive to harm Trish, but possibly killed randomly like a sociopath or psychopath. As thoughts continued flashing through Rossi's mind, he pictured the philosophy professor Trish had been dating. At the time of her murder, Dr. Lawrence Loewenstein appeared to have a motive to kill.

Still looking at the ceiling, Rossi recalled the events leading to his dreaded conversation with Trish's parents at Old Westbury's station house. The morning after Mr. and Mrs. O'Leary heard the devastating news, they flew to New York from their Boston home to meet the detective, learn details of their daughter's murder, and have her body sent home.

Fighting insomnia into the morning's wee hours, the detective conjured a detailed image of the O'Learys. Mr. O'Leary, who looked to be in his early fifties, was dressed in a dark gray suit, pressed white shirt, navy tie, and polished black shoes. His wife appeared to be in her early forties and wore a plain black dress. Her jewelry was simple, with a small gold cross hanging at her chest and a single-strand pearl necklace, complemented by matching pearl earrings. He remembered how Trish's dad controlled his emotions, but his eyes showed strain and worry. Her mom, Rossi recalled, seemed less able to control her feelings, as the whites of her eyes looked red from crying.

As Rossi tried closing his eyes to force sleep, the dialogue with Trish's parents rattled in his head.

"We discovered your daughter's diary in her bottom

desk drawer hidden under a mass of papers. Trish's last entry revealed she was three months pregnant." The detective recalled, just like it was yesterday, what Mrs. O'Leary had asked.

"Do you know the father?"

Rossi remembered replying that the father may have been Dr. Lawrence Loewenstein, a married philosophy professor at the college. Also, Trish wrote in her final entry that the professor had urged her to abort the baby, and she had been disturbed over Loewenstein's lack of empathy when she refused.

"Do you think he murdered our daughter?" Mrs. O'Leary had asked.

"The professor is certainly a person of interest, but we cannot bring him in as a primary murder suspect without first proving her pregnancy. Her diary entry alone is not strong enough incriminating evidence. Before taking Trish home and laying her to rest, an ultrasound test can determine her pregnancy. Six weeks pregnant is the minimum for seeing a fetus, and, according to her diary, Trish was beyond the six-week minimum, though she was not yet showing. With your permission, we must proceed as soon as possible for the best possible imaging."

Mrs. O'Leary wept and cried, "The baby is gone, too!" Her chin trembled as she lashed out at her husband. "If Trish had gone to Marymount College as I wanted, she still would be alive! You're the one who let her do as she pleased!"

Rossi knew Mrs. O'Leary's anger could not change Trish's tragic destiny, and she didn't mean to chastise her husband. It was her hopelessness that caused her to take out her daughter's loss on him.

Finally, after the detective exhausted all his thoughts, he fell asleep. He needed rest to continue investigating the two murders.

Late June 1973: Dr. Loewenstein is Exposed

An ultrasound proved that Trish was pregnant, so her diary entry was enough evidence to signal probable cause for murder. It led to bringing Dr. Loewenstein in for questioning.

Walking into the Old Westbury station house, Loewenstein's thick brown Fu Manchu mustache stood out between his confident grin and brown eyes. His straight, scraggly brown hair, parted on his left, hung to his shoulders. He wore a button-down dungaree shirt, opened wide at the collar and revealing a black T-shirt. His liberal politics and appearance fit the model of a radical activist.

Brought to a room with polygraph equipment, Dr. Loewenstein had to answer tough questions. He was strapped around his chest and arm, with electrodes attached to his fingertips to measure physiological arousal including heart rate, blood pressure, breathing, and perspiration. The experience caused him some paranoia, which showed in his fixed gaze. Then, the polygraph tester administered questions that allowed only a yes or no answer.

"Are you Dr. Lawrence Loewenstein?"

"Yes."

"Are you a philosophy professor at Old Westbury College?"

"Yes."

"Did you first meet Miss O'Leary in your classroom at Old Westbury College?"

"Yes."

"Were you especially friendly with Miss O'Leary?"

"Yes."

"Did you first start getting friendly, beyond the normal student-professor relationship, early in the spring semester of 1973?"

"Yes."

"Did you ever meet Miss O'Leary outside the classroom, either on or off campus?"

"Yes."

"Did you ever meet in a motel or hotel?"

"Yes."

"Did your friendship escalate to a romantic relationship?"

"Yes."

"Was your wife aware of your affair with Miss O'Leary prior to the young girl's death?"

"No."

"Is it true that you had something to hide from your wife? "

"Yes."

"Did you know Miss O'Leary was pregnant when she was murdered?"

"Yes."

"Were you the father?"

"Yes, I believe I was the father."

"In Miss O'Leary's diary entry, she writes about you urging her to get an abortion. Is that true?"

"Yes."

"Did Miss O'Leary react negatively to your urging?"

"Yes and No."

"We require a yes or no response, so I'll rephrase the question. Did Miss O'Leary lean toward not wanting an abortion?"

"Yes."

"Did you ever meet in Miss O'Leary's dormitory room?"

"Yes."

"Did you kill Miss O'Leary in her dormitory room?"

"No, absolutely not!"

"Do you know who did murder Miss O'Leary?"

"No."

That ended the polygraph testing, which Dr. Loewenstein passed. Rossi also learned Loewenstein had an alibi; when Trish was killed, he was on the campus's Great Lawn rallying students to put public pressure on the House of Representatives to impeach

Republican President Richard M. Nixon.

Dr. Loewenstein was absolved from a murder arrest. Though the professor was guilty of cheating on his wife and taking advantage of a vulnerable college girl, he was not a killer. As a result, the case went cold, and it stayed that way going into the fall and winter of 1973.

NINETEEN

RETURNING TO THE SCENE OF THE CRIME

Gibby, the enigmatic and elusive guitarist, unexpectedly returned to Old Westbury College's campus in late January 1974, about one year after he first appeared there. The guitarist returned to retrieve his acoustic Gibson, which he had left behind in the spring of 1973 when forced to abruptly leave the campus after stealing students' property from their dormitory rooms. Gibby hoped all might be forgiven and forgotten, but he still acted nervous back on campus. Though he had changed his appearance by cutting his long hair and shaving his thick mustache, he kept looking over his shoulder and walking very fast.

On his way to the Rathskeller, where Gibby remembered leaving his guitar, he hoped the same bartender was still there. The guitarist smiled when he entered the place and saw the Greek man serving beers, distinguished by his ruffled, white shirt and red vest and salt-and-pepper, waxed handlebar mustache.

"Remember me?" Gibby joked as he extended a hand to the bartender.

Reaching to reciprocate the handshake, the Greek man, though slightly thrown off by Gibby's new appearance, still recognized the guitarist by his droopy left eye.

"Believe I forgot my guitar behind the bar when I left campus last spring."

The bartender bent to get the Gibson. "Have your guitar right here. It's just where you left it. I saved it for you, thinking you might return to claim it one day."

While Gibby tuned his guitar, a student approached the bar. "Can I get a bottle of Heineken, Milo?"

The bartender, on a first name basis with campus regulars, removed the bottle cap to pour the beer into a chilled mug.

"I remember you playing here," the student said to Gibby before sipping the foam on his beer. "Where have you been?"

"Around," he replied shortly. Gibby, preoccupied, didn't want to engage the student. "Is Trish O'Leary still serving tables here?" he asked Milo. The drifter may have asked the question honestly, as he left campus before Trish was killed and perhaps didn't know of her murder. Or, he could have been fishing for information about Trish's case.

"Trish, sadly, was murdered in her dormitory

room last June," the bartender replied, somberly. "I'm surprised you didn't hear the news."

Appearing stunned with his head cast down, Gibby explained that he was far away from campus. "How did it happen?" he asked.

"Some psycho forced his way in and stabbed her multiple times. She didn't have a chance."

The guitarist asked, "Who did it?"

Milo paused to pour himself a shot of Ouzo and slugged it down before answering Gibby's question. "I don't know. It's still an open case."

While Gibby and the bartender stood at the bar reliving memories of Trish, a boisterous group sat around a large wooden table at the back of the Rathskeller. It was Johnny B and his prankster friends. Besides Johnny B, the tie-dyed T-shirt artist, others seated at the table included Roger Boylan, the attractive Jesus-like figure; Sweet Jane, a Mama Cass-type den mother to the group and everybody's lover; and Florence De Flores, a flaming transvestite who sometimes showed up on campus as Johnny B's boyfriend or girlfriend. Even Cole was there as a fringe group member exploring his curious side. Johnny B was leading a conversation about planning a big house party where he and some of his friends had been renting in the town of Huntington, nineteen miles from Old Westbury. The group discussed organizing the party's music, drugs, snacks, and beverages.

Johnny B recognized Gibby tuning his guitar at the bar, despite his new appearance. Cole, who was shocked to see him, turned his back to the bar to avoid being noticed. "Maybe we can get him to play the party," said Johnny B, recalling Gibby's performances at the Rathskeller.

The group's founder walked to the bar to greet the guitar man. "Hey, Gibby! I'm Johnny B. You might have seen me around campus. Everybody knows me by my tie-dyed T-shirts. I saw you perform at the Rathskeller last spring. How would you like to come to a big, off-campus party tonight and entertain everyone? We don't have any money to pay you, but you'll get more drugs than the Grateful Dead."

Gibby laughed at Johnny B's off-handed humor and stopped tuning to think over the offer.

Meanwhile, Cole kept a hidden eye on the guitar player. The young actor knew he had to contact Detective Rossi as soon as possible to tell him about Gibby's whereabouts.

Johnny B continued selling Gibby on coming to the party. "It's going to be a very special night!" said the campus clique's leader with a sly glint in his eye.

"Okay, let's do it!" exclaimed Gibby.

Johnny B agreed to meet Gibby back at the Rathskeller at 7:00 p.m. and drive him to the party. Then, he returned to his table to finalize plans for the bash as Gibby left the campus watering hole.

Afterward, Cole hurried from the Rathskeller to his dormitory room to phone Detective Rossi.

"Detective Rossi. What can I do for you?"

Cole, excited that Rossi picked up the call and thinking faster than he was able to speak, gathered himself. "It's Gavin Cole, detective. Gibby's back!"

Rossi needed details. "Back where? And can you keep him there?"

"Sorry, detective. He was back at the Rathskeller, but I couldn't hold him there. I'm not sure if he's returning to campus, but I know he's supposed to be at a house party tonight in Huntington. There's a particular campus group throwing the party and renting this place."

Detective Rossi knew it was a matter of legally apprehending Gibby at the party to pursue him as a suspect in Trish's murder. He told Gavin to hold the line while he figured out a plan. "I have an idea about how to bring Gibby in for questioning," said the detective when he returned to the line. "I first must get a warrant from a judge to request entry into the house. We'll have to work quickly."

"Will suspicion of murdering Trish justify a warrant?" asked Gavin, who was naïve about the process

"No! Right now, we have zero evidence supporting a case against Gibby for that crime. We can get a warrant to arrest him for attempting to steal property from you and your dormmates last spring, but I'll need you to press charges. Once we pull Gibby in on that charge, we can break him down about Trish's murder."

Rossi got a description of Gibby's new look from

Cole, who was told not to attend the party. The detective didn't want the young actor mixed up in the seizure.

Rossi also noted, from Gavin, the party's location in the Huntington Hills. He learned it was a two-level, stucco house on Tanyard Lane, off the corner of West Neck Road. Gavin didn't remember the house number, but he could provide a description of the place, as he once visited the group members who rented there. He recalled the two-car garage and the second level's large windows with balconies.

Rossi now believed he was on the right trail to cracking Trish's cold case murder.

TWENTY

THE PARTY

That night, everyone living on the block knew the party had started as soon as it got loud. The music was blaring the Grateful Dead, and it didn't take long for a variety of drugs to get passed around the people partying hard. Some were passing a water pipe, smoking a strong hallucinogenic mix of black hashish from Afghanistan with Acapulco Gold weed. Others were snorting lines of uncut cocaine or heroin off a hand mirror through rolled bills.

While the drug scene at the Huntington house party was escalating, Sweet Jane had her eyes on Gibby. She had liked him since she saw him play at the Rathskeller. While he was tuning his guitar on a beat-up sofa chair, preparing to do a set for the doped-up guests, Jane moved closer to the guitarist, like a rock groupie. "Do you want to drop Sunshine with me?" she asked, whispering in his ear.

Gibby felt a rush of excitement, as he anticipated

where this invitation might lead. "Let's go!" he said. "I'm all in with you."

As Gibby and Jane licked the colorless LSD micro dot on blotter paper, three police vehicles quietly rolled up to the stucco house with their headlights off to avoid attention. Stepping from a black, unmarked car were Detective Rossi and Sergeant Reilly. Four other officers got out of two Nassau County police cars. Everyone was armed.

Busted in Huntington

Detective Rossi led his team of officers to the front door and knocked heavily. "Open the door!" he announced through a bullhorn. "We have a warrant to enter the premises and arrest Reno Carson, who goes by Gibby, for attempted theft." When nobody answered the door, as the music drowned out the knocking and command by Rossi, the detective knocked harder and repeated himself even louder.

That time, Johnny B and others close to the front door heard Rossi's pounding and request. However, the group's founder instructed everyone not to answer. He told those within earshot to pass the word about flushing their drugs in the toilets. Everyone was scurrying in a panic to find the bathrooms in the large house.

"One way or another we're coming in, so you might as well open the door," warned Detective Rossi with an ultimatum. He knew the law and explained it concisely:

"If entrance to the house is ignored, the warrant permits us to break open the door or window to gain access."

Johnny B and the party's hosts had run out of time. The house could not be cleared of all drugs. Suddenly, the music stopped, and the tie-dyed artist had to open the door. "What's this about?" he asked, looking and sounding innocent.

"We're here to arrest Reno Carson, commonly known as Gibby, for attempted theft," replied Detective Rossi, showing the warrant. "And we're arresting the renters of this house for drugs seen on site. For now, please show me a copy of the lease. Anyone not on the lease will be free to leave, except Gibby."

The hunted man stood holding his guitar, frozen with heightened paranoia from the acid trip. His droopy left eye was unmistakable to Detective Rossi.

"You're under arrest for attempted theft last spring at Old Westbury College," said Rossi, explaining Gibby's Miranda rights to him. Two officers handcuffed the drifter. It was becoming a bad trip for him.

During the arrest, Johnny B got a copy of the house lease. The artist, Roger Boylan, Sweet Jane, and Florence De Flores were named on the lease, so the foursome was arrested for having various hard drugs on the premises. They were read their Miranda rights, too.

Before getting handcuffed, the four party hosts were asked to empty their pockets in a search for other illegal substances. Several marijuana joints were discovered, adding to the drugs already seized. When

Florence De Flores pulled out a pack of Marlboro Gold from his pocket, Detective Rossi's eyes widened. The detective connected the pack to the one found on Henry's kitchen floor during the crime scene investigation, but he stored the discovery away, waiting for the right time to possibly charge De Flores.

After the party guests had cleared the premises, Reno "Gibby" Carson was led from the house by two officers holding each of his arms. The four campus clique members, who also were handcuffed, followed Gibby to the street. Sergeant Reilly then completed a sweep of the house to ensure no remnants of drugs and drug paraphernalia remained on site. Subsequently, he seized the house keys and locked the door.

While neighbors went to their windows or outside to watch the commotion, Gibby slid into the back seat of Detective Rossi's black car, and Sergeant Reilly put Gibby's Gibson guitar in the vehicle's trunk for safekeeping. Looking out the back window, Gibby watched the four arrested from the campus group get into the back seat of the two patrol cars parked behind Rossi's vehicle. With Detective Rossi leading the way, the vehicles were driven back to Old Westbury's police station. Sergeant Reilly turned to keep a close eye on Gibby, who could soon move from a person of interest to a murder suspect.

TWENTY-ONE

BREAKING DOWN
A SUSPECT

After arriving at the station house, everyone arrested was put in a holding cell until bail could be set the next day at the nearby courthouse. Detective Rossi believed that interrogating Florence De Flores took precedence over questioning the elusive drifter. Besides the Marlboro Gold connection, De Flores's feminine look and big feet raised further suspicion. Those feet appeared to match the large shoe prints found at the crime scenes of Heaton's and Trish's murders.

Rossi took his police captain aside to advise him that he had confiscated the Marlboro Gold cigarette pack from Florence's pants pocket, the same brand found in Heaton's home during the crime scene investigation. The captain, who knew about the incriminating evidence linked to Heaton's murder, chose to be cautious. *It might be wise to wait before making an accusation*, he thought, knowing that Marlboro Gold was a popular brand. Still, the captain was political and ambitious, and he knew that getting a confession could be a game changer for his political goals.

"Did you explain his rights?" asked the captain, addressing Rossi.

"Yes, I did," replied Rossi. "Or, her rights," he added facetiously under his breath.

"Then go for it and get a confession," commanded the captain. "Getting this confession will get you that promotion to lieutenant."

De Flores was seated cross-legged in a plain wooden chair. Looking out the window, he saw only an old, red brick building, adding to the drabness and his worry.

"I got a right to know why you want to question me," demanded De Flores in a throaty voice.

"Again, as I stated in your Miranda rights, you have the right to remain silent and an attorney."

De Flores paused in thought. "Why do I need an attorney? I didn't do anything." Sitting in the hot seat, De Flores waived his rights, as he wanted to show there was nothing to hide.

"So, your name on the lease is Florence," stated Detective Rossi. "Should I call you Florence, then?" Rossi thought his name was unusual, but he was trying to warm up to him and gain his confidence. But Florence, who wasn't opening up, only nodded.

"Have you heard about Henry Heaton, the actor

murdered at his Glen Cove home?"

Squirming in his chair, Florence answered quickly. "Yes, I heard of him. So what?"

"Were you ever at Henry Heaton's house?" asked Rossi.

"Why do you need to know?"

The detective shot back, "I'll ask the questions. You just answer them." Rossi's snarky remark, which instigated the room's younger detectives to rally around him, caused Florence to fold a little.

"Okay, I once went to see Henry. I had seen him around the Old Westbury College campus, and I liked him."

"How did you like him?"

De Flores leaned in, twisting in his chair. "I liked everything about him. You know. He was nice."

Florence was then left alone in another room. An officer gave him a hot cup of coffee for some comfort, and then the officer walked out of the room and locked the door. Sipping his coffee, Florence could only think and face himself in a psychological mirror, part of the process in wearing him down and possibly evoking guilt.

After three hours, the suspect was led back to the interrogation room by the same officer who gave him coffee. Detective Rossi was waiting, ready to step up the inquiry. Florence again sat cross-legged in the sun-washed chair. "Did you visit Heaton late last year on Wednesday, November twenty-first?" asked Rossi.

"I recall it was raining that day."

De Flores began feeling pressured. "Can I get some water?" he asked.

Detective Rossi turned to a young detective in the room. "Get him some water, please," he directed, followed by a pause in the interrogation. As the detective returned with a full glass, Rossi did not miss that De Flores grabbed it with his left hand. Drinking quickly, Florence quenched his thirst and relieved his dry mouth from the bitter coffee and feeling anxious. After he handed the glass back to the detective, the interrogation picked up where it had left off on that rainy day.

"I don't remember the exact day I visited Henry."

Detective Rossi stared at his suspect in the eyes because the eyes never lie, and he held no punches in his interrogation. "We have a witness who said he saw someone leaving Heaton's house on the day he was killed. He said that person looked like a woman. You're dressed as a woman. We think you're involved in Heaton's murder."

"I don't know anything about any murder," countered Florence in defiance.

"We believe you know a lot more than we know."

Though slowly showing signs of breaking, Florence remained in denial. "But I didn't do anything. I already told you."

Detective Rossi lowered his head and stared at Florence's feet. "Stick out your feet," he directed.

"Why should I show my feet?"

Rossi appeared annoyed with De Flores's defiant tone. "Because you look like you have big feet. What size shoe do you wear?" Rossi was sure the suspect's shoe size matched the bloody prints at both crime scenes.

"I'm a twelve D," admitted Florence.

"Confess and you'll feel better," prodded Rossi.

"I believe in live and let live."

"Come on, say it! You killed him. Stabbed him over and over and crushed his skull."

"Okay, okay!" screamed Florence. "I killed him!"

When De Flores vomited from fear, Detective Rossi felt somewhat sorry about his aggressive tactics and softened his tone. "Why did you do it?"

"He saw me! I wish he didn't, because I liked him."

De Flores was talking in riddles, so Rossi kept hammering him. "What do you mean by 'he saw me?'" Although the detective knew exactly what he meant, he had to hear the facts from De Flores. Watching the grilling, the younger detectives were learning from a master interrogator.

"He saw me on campus at the dollhouse as I was leaving the dormitory," revealed De Flores.

"So, what happened in the dormitory?"

"I killed her, too!"

There was silence as the younger detectives looked at each other in astonishment. "Are you saying you murdered Trish O'Leary?" asked Detective Rossi.

"Yes, she's the one. So, I had to kill Henry because

he could testify against me for murdering the girl, if I would be caught and put on trial. I read that newspaper story with Henry's statements. I found his address in the phone book and went to his home; got inside through his bedroom window."

Later, Detective Rossi felt greatly relieved that he was able to induce a double confession, not so much for earning a promotion to lieutenant but because he did his job well. The younger detectives, who had applauded Detective Rossi's work, were able to see he wasn't only the cold-hearted cop who got a confession. Gazing at the overzealous detectives around him, Rossi showed a little lament on his face when he said, "He's psychotic, and they may burn him."

TWENTY-TWO

JUDGEMENT DAY

Shortly after the double confession at the end of
January 1974, a Nassau County district attorney
indicted Florence De Flores for murdering Trish
O'Leary in the first degree. De Flores remained in a
holding cell at Old Westbury's station house until the
trial. Though he had confessed to two murders, the trial
for killing Trish would occur first. An indictment for
killing Henry Heaton would follow only if De Flores
was acquitted for Trish's murder or was released
following a guilty verdict.

The trial, which attracted media attention from
the *Times-Journal* to other local newspapers as well
as TV and radio, began April 1, 1974. It was held in a
courtroom in Mineola, Long Island, where proceedings
had been moved from the neighboring town of Old
Westbury. There was too much emotion and pressure
in Old Westbury for a fair trial, so a change in venue to
Mineola was granted for judicial balance.

The prosecution's opening statement said Miss O'Leary's body was discovered in her dormitory room on June 18, 1973 by a campus maintenance man and carpenter. She had been beaten, bound, and stabbed twenty-one times, and she had lost her unborn baby.

The defense's opening statement was short, as defense attorneys generally believe the less said the better. The public defense attorney, who was heavy set, balding, and wearing a wrinkled suit, simply said Nassau County police revealed that De Flores had previously been in a mental institution, and the defense pleaded not guilty due to insanity.

During the trial, De Flores was either silent, laughing, or talking obscenely. Though the defendant showed his feminine side, he was not his usual flamboyant self, due to required courtroom decorum. He explained some of his actions on that day of the murder but was tight-lipped on details. Responding to the prosecutor and defense attorney, he only divulged how he entered Trish's dormitory room and drugged her.

Then, De Flores was faced with questions from State Supreme Court Justice Daniel D. Gideon, who chose to assert himself in the trial's proceedings; a judge may interrogate the defendant in a murder trial to establish facts and maintain the proceeding's efficiency. Sitting behind a raised bench in his black robe, Judge Gideon symbolized power despite his thin frame. He was focused on getting the truth without delaying the process; his objective was cutting through the tedious proceedings of the prosecution and defense. Though the defense attorney could have objected if the judge's questions appeared inappropriate, there was no pushback.

"Did you kill Trish O'Leary?" asked Judge Gideon.

The defendant slumped in his seat and stared at the jurors. He remained quiet for a minute, and it seemed even longer to jurors who were anxiously anticipating the defendant's answer.

There also was silence among the courtroom's gallery, which included spectators such as Gavin Cole, Detective Rossi, and others who knew Trish from campus. Gibby, who drifted away again after the misdemeanor arrest was dismissed, surprised everyone by showing up for the trial. Apparently, he respected Trish from working with her at the Rathskeller and wanted to see justice done.

The spectators most closely connected to the trial were Mr. and Mrs. O'Leary, Trish's parents. Wanting to keep a low profile to avoid media attention, they sat in the back row of the courtroom holding hands to comfort themselves. They remained transfixed on the trial, listening to every word, even those nearly impossible for them to stomach.

Waiting for De Flores's reply to Judge Gideon's pointed question about killing Trish, many jurors and spectators either fidgeted or sat forward. When De Flores finally spoke, he would not directly answer the judge's question. Instead, he rambled about other details. "I entered the girl's room after I knocked on the door and she opened it. Then, I locked the door, and we talked for a while. In a way, she excited me."

"Are you saying that you liked her sexually?" asked the judge bluntly.

"No! I don't like girls that way." The coroner's examination of Trish confirmed the defendant's reply, as it showed no signs of intercourse.

"So, what did you do?" the judge continued.

"I used my knife once on her."

De Flores was getting closer to admitting murdering Trish, but it seemed he was just tantalizing jurors and courtroom spectators. Then came a number of short, rapid-fire questions from Judge Gideon.

"How did you use the knife?"

"Slit."

"Slit what?"

"Slit her throat."

"What did you do after that?"

"I put my knife aside."

"Was it a fishing or hunting knife?" The judge seemed to be drawing out De Flores.

"Hunting." The defendant then explained getting a smaller knife and stabbing Trish all over her body, gesturing those actions dramatically to seek attention. De Flores could not recount how many times he stabbed her—claiming he just kept going until his arm could no longer keep up with the hate in his head. "She called me a pig as I stabbed her."

"How did that make you feel?"

"I felt rage." A sardonic smile came over the defendant.

"Did you kill because she teased you about how you dressed?"

"No."

"Then why?"

"I just like to kill."

"Why do you like killing?"

"I get satisfaction from it."

The defendant's responses stunned the jurors and gallery. The shock could be read on their faces. For some, their eyes widened and eyebrows raised. For others, their mouths hung open. Even Judge Gideon, who was used to presiding over trials prosecuting cold-hearted murderers, appeared aghast.

After those questions, the judge called for a short recess. De Flores was moved from the courtroom to the antechamber to meet with his attorney. Everyone in the courtroom could hear the chilling clinking of his hand and leg chains as he hobbled out.

When De Flores and his attorney returned to the courtroom for a final time, Judge Gideon concluded questioning the defendant.

"What did you do after the killing?"

"I was covered with blood, so I looked for a place to wash. Found a bathroom on the same floor as the girl's room. It was a women's bathroom, but that didn't matter to me. Anyway, nobody saw me there."

"Then what?"

"I left her dormitory to go home through that pine forest. But just before I passed the campus swimming pool, I saw that actor looking at me near the dollhouse. At the time, I didn't realize he would become a big problem for me."

The judge completed his questioning, followed by closing arguments. The prosecution made it clear that De Flores's actions were premeditated, and he was in his right mind. Thus, the jury was certain of the defendant's guilt.

Because he may have been insane at the time of the murder, the defense, as in its plea at the trial's start, pushed for a verdict of not guilty by reason of insanity. The defense emphasized, once again, that De Flores's earlier release from a mental institution along with his outrageous words and actions during the trial had proved it.

When the verdict came in from the jury, De Flores was found guilty but mentally ill. This alternative to an insanity defense meant that although the defendant was viewed as mentally ill, he was not severely ill enough to be found not guilty due to insanity.

Following the verdict, loud cheers could be heard from the gallery, believing justice had been served. Mr. and Mrs. O'Leary wept in the back of the courtroom, with mixed emotions of sadness for their daughter and satisfaction that she had received justice.

Judge Gideon scheduled sentencing for Monday, April, 22 but he curiously changed the date to Tuesday, April 23, because of De Flores's strange request. The convicted killer wanted to watch the Monday night movie, Hitchcock's *Psycho*, on television.

On sentencing day, the judge faced De Flores to explain the logic and arrangement for his penalty. "A guilty verdict, even though you have been declared mentally ill, means you are criminally liable. As a result, you will be sent to Pilgrim State Hospital, a mental institution on Long Island, where you will be imprisoned in its jail and required to receive psychiatric treatment. If and when you are cured of your mental illness, you will be sent to a New York State maximum-security prison, named at that time, to carry out a life sentence."

The convicted Florence De Flores was taken from the courtroom in leg and hand chains to a highly-secured holding cell, where he would wait to be moved to Pilgrim State. On his way out of the courtroom, he smirked and laughed and sashayed. All in attendance had their eyes on him, and that attention was just what De Flores wanted!

TWENTY-THREE

PILGRIM STATE

Florence De Flores wore leg and hand chains as he was moved from his holding cell to Pilgrim State, the same psychiatric institution where the Hammerhead Killer had been confined for the Planting Fields serial murders of 1967. Like him, De Flores had a secret dark side that even his sometimes boyfriend, Johnny B, did not detect.

On his way into the facility, where he would be jailed and treated for mental illness, he was accompanied by two correction officers, one on each side of him. They were holding the convicted killer by his arms and slow-walking him due to the physical limitations of his leg chains. As they got closer to the iron entrance gate, two additional officers were seen holding long rifles and guarding the entrance.

At the gate, De Flores paused and stared at the institution's name, *Pilgrim State Hospital*, carved at the top of it in large, block lettering. Then, he turned to the correction officers accompanying him and said, "That looks like electrified wire along the top of the fence surrounding the grounds." In that moment, he thought, *there may be no way out of here.* Though the mental patient probably did not realize it, his thinking had a double meaning: He may be forever trapped in his own mind.

One of the sentinels then unlocked the gate and swung it open, and ominous signs could be seen on the other side of it. As the two correction officers continued walking De Flores through the opened gate, the killer eyed a skinny male patient in leg and hand chains like himself. He was wearing a gray, button-down shirt and loose-fitting gray pants, and he was meticulously gathering branches that had fallen during the previous night's storm. De Flores felt the winds against his face and watched the branches blowing around the grounds. The skinny patient clumsily chased the branches, making sure that he put each one in a black garbage bag. *This man's behavior seems obsessive,* thought De Flores. *If they cannot help him, how can they help me? Nobody gets cured.*

As he was escorted across the grounds, De Flores became transfixed on another strange-looking patient. She was a frail older woman dressed in a gray, shapeless shift with large buttons. The patient had scraggly hair, rotten teeth, and a glassy look in her eyes. She stared and winked at De Flores. *Why is she winking at me?* he asked himself, feeling perplexed by her creepy action.

Perhaps she is just welcoming the new kid to the block.

After being admitted to the psychiatric division, De Flores was hosed down and dressed in the same gray uniform as all the other male patients and taken to Building 21. The building housed cells for the most dangerous male patients.

Concerned about suicidal patients, the hospital's authority locked De Flores in a concrete-walled, padded cell with a cushioned floor. It was forty-eight square feet, just enough space for basic necessities: a bed, toilet, and sink. Built into the cell's door was a small window made of thick glass that could not be penetrated. It was used for observing mentally ill prisoners, like De Flores, who might be suicidal.

De Flores felt the cell's small size limited his movement, and having no window cut him off from the outside world. *I'm feeling claustrophobic*, he thought. *The cell seems to be spinning.* He became dizzy and nauseous, which were the first signs of his panic attack.

In addition to being confined, De Flores had been deprived of his makeup, nail polish, and frilly clothes. He was anxious about feeling uncomfortable in his own skin, an imprisonment of another kind. He cringed as his anxiety worsened.

That first night, De Flores sat on his bed and thought about his past and what had led him to this horrible place. He drifted back to his early childhood as a pre-teen and became delusional remembering his mother, whose face transformed into Trish's face.

Several days later, De Flores's cell door was opened by a corrections officer, who summoned him to see Dr. Goodman, one of the hospital's top psychiatrists dedicated to helping mental patients. De Flores was taken, in hand and leg chains, to the psychiatric center.

As he was being led from Building 21, the killer heard the scream of a longtime patient, whose cell door had been opened by another corrections officer. "Don't let them take you to the tower to drill into your brain, as they did to me!" The patient had experienced a frontal lobe lobotomy, the same gruesome treatment, according to legend, performed on the Hammerhead Killer to dull his erratic behavior.

Nearing Dr. Goodman's office in the psychiatric center, De Flores observed the walls constructed of ten-inch by five-inch yellow tiles. In chromotherapy, the color yellow is meant to soothe the mind. Some of the patients he saw looked tranquil, subdued by drugs. De Flores noticed the hospital's nursing staff, dressed all in white, cajoling patients.

Facing the Demons

At Dr. Goodman's office door, the corrections officer knocked and announced that his patient was ready. Dr. Goodman opened the door cautiously, then cheerfully said, "Step inside my office." The psychiatrist looked at Florence in a friendly manner, trying to connect with him at first sight. Then the doctor turned to the corrections officer. "Please remove his hand and leg chains," he said. "I'll take over from here." Subsequently, the doctor dismissed the corrections officer until De Flores would be ready to return to his cell.

"Have a seat on the sofa," said Dr. Goodman, inviting Florence to relax so he would loosen up and talk. "Would you like a cigarette?" he asked in an effort to bond with Florence. "I have Marlboro Gold."

"Sure, that's my brand."

The psychiatrist gave his patient a cigarette and lit it for him before offering an ashtray. It was no coincidence that the doctor happened to have a pack of Marlboro Gold. He had done his research prior to talking with De Flores, but there was more to learn, if the patient was to improve through psychiatric treatment. The doctor needed to delve much deeper into De Flores's past and the motivations that drove him.

"I'm going to give you an injection," said Dr. Goodman. "It will help me to help you, so you need to trust me."

De Flores, a little reluctant of the unknown, questioned the doctor. "Will it hurt?" Then he dragged on the cigarette to calm his anxiety.

Dr. Goodman thought, *how ironic a question, given his compulsion to inflict pain on others.* "You'll feel no pain; just a pinch."

De Flores motioned to his left arm in agreement, as Dr. Goodman told him to lie down. After finding a vein, the doctor injected him with sodium pentothal, more commonly known as a truth serum. The drug, which suppresses brain inhibition, was believed to encourage psychotic patients to talk more freely.

As De Flores started feeling woozy, with a hypnotizing effect coming over him, he turned to look out a barred window. He was mesmerized by the hard and steady rain, like the rain on the stormy night just before he entered Pilgrim State, and months earlier when he killed Henry Heaton. Suddenly, Florence saw a bolt of lightning that lit up the sky, triggering his fear. He turned to Dr. Goodman. "Are you taking me to the tower?" De Flores candidly asked about what he had been fearing.

"No. We closed the tower some years ago." Dr. Goodman had been one of the nation's psychiatrists leading the trend of transitioning to kinder and gentler therapies such as using drugs and implementing more refined moral care of patients.

After the psychiatrist relieved Florence's fear, he set out to explore the roots of his patient's mental problems. "I would like to start by talking to you about your life, Florence," said Dr. Goodman.

"What about my life? It's a life like anybody's life."

"Let's go back to when you were very young. What do you remember about your first toys?"

Feeling less inhibited, De Flores began talking, as the truth serum was working through his bloodstream. "Oh, sure. I had a teddy bear and some dolls. They were soft and cuddly dolls that I would sleep with, along with my bear."

"Did you have boy or girl dolls?" asked Dr. Goodman.

"I had one of each. I was given a Raggedy Ann and a Raggedy Andy that were brother and sister."

Trying to better relate with his patient, the doctor acknowledged that he remembered those dolls' popularity. "A lot of children had those dolls. Did you have other toys?"

"On my sixth birthday, I received a doctor's kit, and I liked playing doctor with the other children. I had no interest in toy trains and work tools for kids like other boys my age." Then, Florence began getting skeptical. "But why are you asking these questions?"

Dr. Goodman paused, as he had to be thoughtful about not probing too hard, which might cause Florence to go quiet. "I'm just trying to know you better at the beginning of your childhood, so I can understand how and why your life developed as it did," he replied.

"Then, what else can we discuss?" asked De Flores.

Dr. Goodman envisioned Florence dressing femininely around Old Westbury College, as he was one-of-a-kind on campus in 1973. The doctor wondered how the cross-dressing started. "Do you remember what you wore when you were very young?"

"I wore flannel nightgowns, starting when I was five. I slept in those nightgowns."

"What daytime clothes did you wear at that age? For example, did you wear overalls like many young boys and girls?"

Florence's reply was telling. "There were no overalls. Around the house, I wore dresses. That's how my mother dressed me. And I wore sandals and ballet slippers; no sneakers like the other kids."

"What did your dad say about you wearing dresses?"

Florence went silent. "I don't want to talk about that now."

Dr. Goodman didn't want to push his patient, so he pivoted to ease into talking about Florence's father. "Can you remember your first haircut?"

Florence loved his flowing hair, so he wanted to open up again. "I don't recall my father taking me to the barber. I wore my hair long, and my mother trimmed it when it grew too much."

"Can we talk in general about your dad?" asked the doctor, slowly trying to learn about the father's reaction to Florence wearing dresses.

"My dad was a big guy whose face was scratchy."

Realization came over the doctor. "How would you remember that his face was scratchy?"

Florence winced, then replied sheepishly, "He would come into my room when I was wearing dresses. Sometimes my dad would rub my back, and then he would do more."

"What more?"

Again, Florence stopped short, but Dr. Goodman understood how the dresses wrongly tempted Florence's father. The doctor raised a final question before ending his first treatment. "What did your mother say or do when your father came into your room?"

Florence quickly got angry. "She turned her back on me and looked the other way, as if nothing was happening. I hated my mother for that, and any woman who reminded me of her."

Dr. Goodman saw that the sodium pentothal was wearing off, as Florence no longer looked glazed, so he thought it was the right time to end his first session. The doctor knew that pushing too hard could be self-defeating.

Florence was taken back, in leg and hand chains, to his cell in Building 21 by the same corrections officer who summoned him from there. Though Florence was returning to confinement, he welcomed the familiarity of his corrections officer. He also liked talking to Dr. Goodman, who gave him a sense of relief. Truth revealed that Florence's first treatment was the start of facing his demons, but he had a long way to go before Dr. Goodman could stabilize his hatred and dangerous actions. While De Flores's treatments continued, he disappeared into Pilgrim State Hospital.

Some who knew about him, especially Detective Rossi, questioned his mental state in confinement. Maybe Florence would eventually be set free from his demons and cured of his mental illness, but surely the man who had been conflicted and appeared to enjoy killing would be locked up for life, either at Pilgrim

State or a maximum-security prison in New York State. That was his destiny. Though born innocent, De Flores's future had been shaped by his early childhood experiences and the parents controlling them.

ABOUT THE AUTHOR

Gary M. Cianci, a former business journalist, public relations executive, and college instructor, had his first novel, *Brothers of Brooklyn*, published in January 2022. His second novel, *The Final Act*, was inspired by a true story that he personally experienced in 1973.

Gary lives in Bay Ridge, Brooklyn with his wife, Anna Patricia, and their dog. He enjoys spending time with his two daughters.

When not writing, Gary avidly follows baseball, watches old movies, and listens to music such as American standards, classic rock, and jazz.

The author welcomes communications and can be reached at GaryCianci@aol.com.